THE TIME AND THE PLACE and Other Stories

Naguib Mahfouz

THE TIME AND THE PLACE and Other Stories

Selected and Translated by

Denys Johnson-Davies

The American University in Cairo Press

113 Sharia Kasr el Aini
Cairo, Egypt
www.aucpress.com

First paperback edition 1995
Third printing 2001

Dar el Kutub No. 5777/95
ISBN 977 424 374 9

Printed in Egypt

Contents

CONTENTS

Introduction

It is of course as a novelist that Naguib Mahfouz is best known. His output in that field, nearly forty books, is by any standard formidable and inevitably overshadows his accomplishments as a writer of short stories. And yet his fourteen volumes of short stories contain some of the best in modern Arabic literature—and it is the short story which, in the Arab world, has been the preferred genre since the first attempts at writing fiction in Arabic were made early in this century. (Let us ignore here the fact that one of the world's greatest masterpieces of fiction, *A Thousand and One Nights*, was composed in Arabic.) Short stories by Naguib Mahfouz have appeared in translation in many languages, and it is interesting to find, in a collection such as *The Art of the Tale* (Penguin, 1986), alongside the work of such authors as Borges, Beckett, Camus, Greene, and Marquez, a single example from the Arab world—a story by Naguib Mahfouz, and this before he had been awarded the Nobel Prize. The story chosen is "The Conjurer Made Off with the Dish," which had previously been published in a collection of stories by Egyptian writers and is included in the present volume. Of the remaining nineteen stories in this volume, all but three are appearing in English for the first time.

Naguib Mahfouz is essentially an Egyptian writer. Born in 1911 in Gamaliyya, one of Cairo's most picturesque districts, he has spent his life in that city and moves from it only once a year, to spend the hot summer months in seaside Alexandria. Only twice in his life has he been abroad, and after his second trip he vowed never to travel again. His writings, almost without exception, are placed in Cairo; in the present collection only "A Day for Saying Goodbye" has another setting—Alexandria. Like their author, his stories never travel abroad, not even to the Egyptian countryside with its peasant life, which has been such fertile soil for most Egyptian writers. A predominance of his novels and stories are sited in that square mile or so which makes up the districts of Gamaliyya and al-Hussein, an area which includes that vast bazaar known to tourists as Khan al-Khalili, with its numerous mosques, cafés, small shops, and jostling motley of colorful characters.

Stories like "Fear" and "The Wasteland" take place in the dark narrow alleyways of bustling activity where *fitiwwat*—"toughs," the bosses of small gangs—contend for control of some area of a quarter and exploit it to their advantage. (Today the *fitiwwat*, like the gangsters of the days of Prohibition, are a thing of the past.) Both these early stories also show Naguib Mahfouz's preoccupation with time—he has cited Proust as one of his main literary influences. In "The Wasteland" the protagonist's single-minded efforts are rendered meaningless by his failure to take account of the fact that, for others as much as for himself, time accompanies people on their journey through life. In "Fear," too, by the end of the story time has stolen the bloom of youth from Na'ima's cheeks and has given the dashing young police officer a paunch. "The Empty Café" tells of the loneliness of old age: a long life, as the old man says, is a curse. It is as though he no longer belongs to the human race, having outstripped all his contemporaries, and ends by hoping to find companionship in another species, the cat belonging to his young, over-rambunctious grandson. "A Long-Term Plan" reminds us that nothing in life is right unless its timing is right, no good luck so futile as when it comes at the wrong time. Most moving of all the stories concerned with time is the short "Half a Day," where time is telescoped into the morning's walk, the first day at school, and the return journey home. It is a gentle story tinged with nostalgia for time irrecoverable.

In the West, as religion becomes increasingly a social function or merely part of the cultural background, many people like to think that, helped by such institutions as insurance companies, they are masters of their fate. The East, particularly the Islamic East, knows better. The Koran tells the Muslim that a person's life span lies in God's hands, emphasizing that every soul must taste death. Not surprisingly, death plays a leading role in the lives of the characters that people Naguib Mahfouz's writings.

The period from 1967 to 1971, following Egypt's disastrous 1967 war with Israel, was a bad one for Mahfouz. During those dark years he gave up writing novels and turned to the short story. In many of the stories he wrote during this time—among his best and blackest—death is central. Referring to these stories, he has remarked that he could never conquer the idea of dying until he wrote about it. Stories like "At the Bus Stop" are as bleakly pessimistic as anything he has written. "A Fugitive from Justice" contains a very short scene, quite extraneous to the events of the story, in which the funeral procession of a young girl prompts one of the protagonists to observe: "Isn't it the road we all take?" Such reminders crop up often in Mahfouz's stories.

In "The Man and the Other Man," the world is described as being subject to many laws, not just one—and several of the stories in this volume inhabit that gray area that lies behind the façade of comfortable reality. "Zaabalawi," for instance, introduces us to a world of uncertainty, frustration, and contradiction, a world inspired by Sufism, Islam's particular brand of mysticism, in whose rich literature Naguib Mahfouz is deeply read. In "The Time and the Place," the author, with great deftness, creates a Thousand-and-One-Nights atmosphere and prepares his reader for—and makes credible—happenings that can only be explained in terms of some super-natural law. All this he does with a remarkable economy of words. This ability to be brief and explicit Mahfouz ascribes to the many film scenarios he has written during his career.

Modern Arabic literature as a whole contains little humor, though the Egyptians especially are noted for their wit and their habit of making fun of their circumstances and, in particular, of their leaders. Some of this dry humor is to be found in "The Norwegian Rat," as well as in "The Ditch," which deals with the economic tribulations of middle-class Egyptians living in a society crippled by inflation and suffering such an acute housing shortage that many have in desperation taken up residence in the family mausoleums in the "City of the Dead."

The slight and somewhat uncharacteristic story "The Answer Is No" is Naguib Mahfouz's most recent. At the time he was awarded the Nobel Prize, an Egyptian weekly asked him for any recent story that was as yet unpublished, and he sent them this one. What is remarkable about it is that, written by a man of his generation, it should be so outspokenly feminist. For the Western reader it provides an insight into how different Eastern societies are in respect of sexual mores, even a country as modern-minded as Egypt. A Western reader might well ask, "What's all the fuss about?" Naguib Mahfouz, as an Egyptian, knows what the fuss is about but makes it clear where his own sympathies lie.

It was in 1934, the year in which he graduated in philosophy from Cairo University, that Mahfouz saw published his first piece of original writing—a short story. At that time, he would send his stories to magazines and be delighted if they appeared in print. He recounts how one day an editor asked him to call round at his office. He did so and was handed a pound for his latest story. "One gets paid for them as well!" exclaimed the budding writer in disbelief—and it was with the same modest disbelief that, more than half a century later, he received the news of the Nobel Prize.

DENYS JOHNSON-DAVIES

THE TIME AND THE PLACE and Other Stories

Zaabalawi

Finally I became convinced that I had to find Sheikh Zaabalawi.

The first time I had heard his name had been in a song:

> *Oh what's become of the world, Zaabalawi?*
> *They've turned it upside down and taken away its taste.*

It had been a popular song in my childhood, and one day it had occurred to me to demand of my father, in the way children have of asking endless questions:

"Who is Zaabalawi?"

He had looked at me hesitantly as though doubting my ability to understand the answer. However, he had replied, "May his blessing descend upon you, he's a true saint of God, a remover of worries and troubles. Were it not for him I would have died miserably—"

In the years that followed, I heard my father many a time sing the praises of this good saint and speak of the miracles he performed. The days passed and brought with them many illnesses, for each one of which I was able, without too much trouble and at a cost I could afford, to find a cure, until I became afflicted with that illness for which no one possesses a remedy. When I had tried everything in vain and was overcome by despair, I remembered by chance what I had heard in my childhood: Why, I asked myself, should I not seek out Sheikh Zaabalawi? I recollected my father saying that he had made his acquaintance in Khan Gaafar at the house of Sheikh Qamar, one of those sheikhs who practiced law in the religious courts, and so I took myself off to his house. Wishing to make sure that he was still living there, I made inquiries of a vendor of beans whom I found in the lower part of the house.

"Sheikh Qamar!" he said, looking at me in amazement. "He left the quarter ages ago. They say he's now living in Garden City and has his office in al-Azhar Square."

I looked up the office address in the telephone book and immediately set off to the Chamber of Commerce Building, where it was located. On asking to see Sheikh Qamar, I was ushered into a room just as a beautiful woman with a most intoxicating perfume was leaving it. The man received me with a smile and motioned me toward a fine leather-upholstered chair. Despite the thick soles of my shoes, my feet were conscious of the lushness of the costly carpet. The man wore a lounge suit and was smoking a cigar; his manner of sitting was that of someone well satisfied both with himself and with his worldly possessions. The look of warm welcome he gave me left no doubt in my mind that he thought me a prospective client, and I felt acutely embarrassed at encroaching upon his valuable time.

"Welcome!" he said, prompting me to speak.

"I am the son of your old friend Sheikh Ali al-Tatawi," I answered so as to put an end to my equivocal position.

A certain languor was apparent in the glance he cast at me; the languor was not total in that he had not as yet lost all hope in me.

"God rest his soul," he said. "He was a fine man."

The very pain that had driven me to go there now prevailed upon me to stay.

"He told me," I continued, "of a devout saint named Zaabalawi whom he met at Your Honor's. I am in need of him, sir, if he be still in the land of the living."

The languor became firmly entrenched in his eyes, and it would have come as no surprise if he had shown the door to both me and my father's memory.

"That," he said in the tone of one who has made up his mind to terminate the conversation, "was a very long time ago and I scarcely recall him now."

Rising to my feet so as to put his mind at rest regarding my intention of going, I asked, "Was he really a saint?"

"We used to regard him as a man of miracles."

"And where could I find him today?" I asked, making another move toward the door.

"To the best of my knowledge he was living in the Birgawi Residence in al-Azhar," and he applied himself to some papers on his desk with a resolute movement that indicated he would not open his mouth again. I bowed my head in thanks, apologized several times for disturbing him, and left the office, my head so buzzing with embarrassment that I was oblivious to all sounds around me.

I went to the Birgawi Residence, which was situated in a thickly populated quarter. I found that time had so eaten away at the building that nothing was left of it save an antiquated façade and a courtyard that, despite being supposedly in the charge of a caretaker, was being used as a rubbish dump. A small, insignificant fellow, a mere prologue to a man, was using the covered entrance as a place for the sale of old books on theology and mysticism.

When I asked him about Zaabalawi, he peered at me through narrow, inflamed eyes and said in amazement, "Zaabalawi! Good heavens, what a time ago that was! Certainly he used to live in this house when it was habitable. Many were the times he would sit with me talking of bygone days, and I would be blessed by his holy presence. Where, though, is Zaabalawi today?"

He shrugged his shoulders sorrowfully and soon left me, to attend to an approaching customer. I proceeded to make inquiries of many shopkeepers in the district. While I found that a large number of them had never even heard of Zaabalawi, some, though recalling nostalgically the pleasant times they had spent with him, were ignorant of his present whereabouts, while others openly made fun of him, labeled him a charlatan, and advised me to put myself in the hands of a doctor—as though I had not already done so. I therefore had no alternative but to return disconsolately home.

With the passing of days like motes in the air, my pains grew so severe that I was sure I would not be able to hold out much longer. Once again I fell to wondering about Zaabalawi and clutching at the hope his venerable name stirred within me. Then it occurred to me to seek the help of the local sheikh of the district; in fact, I was surprised I had not thought of this to begin with. His office was in the nature of a small shop, except that it contained a desk and a telephone, and I found him sitting at his desk, wearing a jacket over his striped galabeya. As he did not interrupt his conversation with a man sitting beside him, I stood waiting till the man had gone. The sheikh then looked up at me coldly. I told myself that I should win him over by the usual methods, and it was not long before I had him cheerfully inviting me to sit down.

"I'm in need of Sheikh Zaabalawi," I answered his inquiry as to the purpose of my visit.

He gazed at me with the same astonishment as that shown by those I had previously encountered.

"At least," he said, giving me a smile that revealed his gold teeth, "he is still alive. The devil of it is, though, he has no fixed abode. You might well bump into him as you go out of here, on the other hand you might spend days and months in fruitless searching."

"Even you can't find him!"

"Even I! He's a baffling man, but I thank the Lord that he's still alive!"

He gazed at me intently, and murmured, "It seems your condition is serious."

"Very."

"May God come to your aid! But why don't you go about it systematically?" He spread out a sheet of paper on the desk and drew on it with unexpected speed and skill until he had made a full plan of the district, showing all the various quarters, lanes, alleyways, and squares. He looked at it admiringly and said, "These are dwelling-houses, here is the Quarter of the Perfumers, here the Quarter of the Coppersmiths, the Mouski, the police and fire stations. The drawing is your best guide. Look carefully in the cafés, the places where the dervishes perform their rites, the mosques and prayer-rooms, and the Green Gate, for he may well be concealed among the beggars and be indistinguishable from them. Actually, I myself haven't seen him for years, having been somewhat preoccupied with the cares of the world, and was only brought back by your inquiry to those most exquisite times of my youth."

I gazed at the map in bewilderment. The telephone rang, and he took up the receiver.

"Take it," he told me, generously. "We're at your service."

Folding up the map, I left and wandered off through the quarter, from square to street to alleyway, making inquiries of everyone I felt was familiar with the place. At last the owner of a small establishment for ironing clothes told me, "Go to the calligrapher Hassanein in Umm al-Ghulam—they were friends."

I went to Umm al-Ghulam, where I found old Hassanein working in a deep, narrow shop full of signboards and jars of color. A strange smell, a mixture of glue and perfume, permeated its every corner. Old Hassanein was squatting on a sheepskin rug in front of a board propped against the wall; in the middle of it he had inscribed the word "Allah" in silver lettering. He was engrossed in embellishing the letters with prodigious care. I stood behind him, fearful of disturbing him or breaking the inspiration that flowed to his masterly hand. When my concern at not interrupting him had lasted some time, he suddenly inquired with unaffected gentleness, "Yes?"

Realizing that he was aware of my presence, I introduced myself. "I've been told that Sheikh Zaabalawi is your friend; I'm looking for him," I said.

His hand came to a stop. He scrutinized me in astonishment. "Zaabalawi! God be praised!" he said with a sigh.

"He *is* a friend of yours, isn't he?" I asked eagerly.

"He was, once upon a time. A real man of mystery: he'd visit you so often that people would imagine he was your nearest and dearest, then would disappear as though he'd never existed. Yet saints are not to be blamed."

The spark of hope went out with the suddenness of a lamp snuffed by a power-cut.

"He was so constantly with me," said the man, "that I felt him to be a part of everything I drew. But where is he today?"

"Perhaps he is still alive?"

"He's alive, without a doubt. . . . He had impeccable taste, and it was due to him that I made my most beautiful drawings."

"God knows," I said, in a voice almost stifled by the dead ashes of hope, "how dire my need for him is, and no one knows better than you of the ailments in respect to which he is sought."

"Yes, yes. May God restore you to health. He is in truth, as is said of him, a man, and more. . . ."

Smiling broadly, he added, "And his face possesses an unforgettable beauty. But where is he?"

Reluctantly I rose to my feet, shook hands, and left. I continued wandering eastward and westward through the quarter, inquiring about Zaabalawi from everyone who, by reason of age or experience, I felt might be likely to help me. Eventually I was informed by a vendor of lupine that he had met him a short while ago at the house of Sheikh Gad, the well-known composer. I went to the musician's house in Tabakshiyya, where I found him in a room tastefully furnished in the old style, its walls redolent with history. He was seated on a divan, his famous lute beside him, concealing within itself the most beautiful melodies of our age, while somewhere from within the house came the sound of pestle and mortar and the clamor of children. I immediately greeted him and introduced myself, and was put at my ease by the unaffected way in which he received me. He did not ask, either in words or gesture, what had brought me, and I did not feel that he even harbored any such curiosity. Amazed at his understanding and kindness, which boded well, I said, "O Sheikh Gad, I am an admirer of yours, having long been enchanted by the renderings of your songs."

"Thank you," he said with a smile.

"Please excuse my disturbing you," I continued timidly, "but I was told that Zaabalawi was your friend, and I am in urgent need of him."

"Zaabalawi!" he said, frowning in concentration. "You need him? God be with you, for who knows, O Zaabalawi, where you are."

"Doesn't he visit you?" I asked eagerly.

"He visited me some time ago. He might well come right now; on the other hand I mightn't see him till death!"

I gave an audible sigh and asked, "What made him like that?"

The musician took up his lute. "Such are saints or they would not be saints," he said, laughing.

"Do those who need him suffer as I do?"

"Such suffering is part of the cure!"

He took up the plectrum and began plucking soft strains from the strings. Lost in thought, I followed his movements. Then, as though addressing myself, I said, "So my visit has been in vain."

He smiled, laying his cheek against the side of the lute. "God forgive you," he said, "for saying such a thing of a visit that has caused me to know you and you me!"

I was much embarrassed and said apologetically, "Please forgive me; my feelings of defeat made me forget my manners."

"Do not give in to defeat. This extraordinary man brings fatigue to all who seek him. It was easy enough with him in the old days, when his place of abode was known. Today, though, the world has changed, and after having enjoyed a position attained only by potentates, he is now pursued by the police on a charge of false pretenses. It is therefore no longer an easy matter to reach him, but have patience and be sure that you will do so."

He raised his head from the lute and skillfully fingered the opening bars of a melody. Then he sang:

"I make lavish mention, even though I blame myself,
of those I love,
For the stories of the beloved are my wine."

With a heart that was weary and listless, I followed the beauty of the melody and the singing.

"I composed the music to this poem in a single night," he told me when he had finished. "I remember that it was the eve of the Lesser Bairam. Zaabalawi was my guest for the whole of that night, and the poem was of his choosing. He would sit for a while just where you are, then would get up and play with my children as though he were one of them. Whenever I was overcome by weariness or my inspiration failed me, he would punch me playfully in the chest and joke with me, and I would bubble over with melodies, and thus I continued working till I finished the most beautiful piece I have ever composed."

"Does he know anything about music?"

"He is the epitome of things musical. He has an extremely beautiful speaking voice, and you have only to hear him to want to burst into song and to be inspired to creativity. . . ."

"How was it that he cured those diseases before which men are powerless?"

"That is his secret. Maybe you will learn it when you meet him."

But when would that meeting occur? We relapsed into silence, and the hubbub of children once more filled the room.

Again the sheikh began to sing. He went on repeating the words "and I have a memory of her" in different and beautiful variations until the very walls danced in ecstasy. I expressed my wholehearted admiration, and he gave me a smile of thanks. I then got up and asked permission to leave, and he accompanied me to the front door. As I shook him by the hand, he said, "I hear that nowadays he frequents the house of Hagg Wanas al-Damanhouri. Do you know him?"

I shook my head, though a modicum of renewed hope crept into my heart.

"He is a man of private means," the sheikh told me, "who from time to time visits Cairo, putting up at some hotel or other. Every evening, though, he spends at the Negma Bar in Alfi Street."

I waited for nightfall and went to the Negma Bar. I asked a waiter about Hagg Wanas, and he pointed to a corner that was semisecluded because of its position behind a large pillar with mirrors on all four sides. There I saw a man seated alone at a table with two bottles in front of him, one empty, the other two-thirds empty. There were no snacks or food to be seen, and I was sure that I was in the presence of a hardened drinker. He was wearing a loosely flowing silk galabeya and a carefully wound turban; his legs were stretched out toward the base of the pillar, and as he gazed into the mirror in rapt contentment, the sides of his face, rounded and handsome despite the fact that he was approaching old age, were flushed with wine. I approached quietly till I stood but a few feet away from him. He did not turn toward me or give any indication that he was aware of my presence.

"Good evening, Mr. Wanas," I greeted him cordially.

He turned toward me abruptly, as though my voice had roused him from slumber, and glared at me in disapproval. I was about to explain what had brought me when he interrupted in an almost imperative tone of voice that was nonetheless not devoid of an extraordinary gentleness, "First, please sit down, and second, please get drunk!"

I opened my mouth to make my excuses, but, stopping up his ears with his fingers, he said, "Not a word till you do what I say."

I realized I was in the presence of a capricious drunkard and told myself that I should at least humor him a bit. "Would you permit me to ask one question?" I said with a smile, sitting down.

Without removing his hands from his ears he indicated the bottle. "When engaged in a drinking bout like this, I do not allow any conversation between myself and another unless, like me, he is drunk, otherwise all propriety is lost and mutual comprehension is rendered impossible."

I made a sign indicating that I did not drink.

"That's your lookout," he said offhandedly. "And that's my condition!"

He filled me a glass, which I meekly took and drank. No sooner had the wine settled in my stomach than it seemed to ignite. I waited patiently till I had grown used to its ferocity, and said, "It's very strong, and I think the time has come for me to ask you about—"

Once again, however, he put his fingers in his ears. "I shan't listen to you until you're drunk!"

He filled up my glass for the second time. I glanced at it in trepidation; then, overcoming my inherent objection, I drank it down at a gulp. No sooner had the wine come to rest inside me than I lost all willpower. With the third glass, I lost my memory, and with the fourth the future vanished. The world turned round about me, and I forgot why I had gone there. The man leaned toward me attentively, but I saw him—saw everything—as a mere meaningless series of colored planes. I don't know how long it was before my head sank down onto the arm of the chair and I plunged into deep sleep. During it, I had a beautiful dream the like of which I had never experienced. I dreamed that I was in an immense garden surrounded on all sides by luxuriant trees, and the sky was nothing but stars seen between the entwined branches, all enfolded in an atmosphere like that of sunset or a sky overcast with cloud. I was lying on a small hummock of jasmine petals, more of which fell upon me like rain, while the lucent spray of a fountain unceasingly sprinkled the crown of my head and my temples. I was in a state of deep contentedness, of ecstatic serenity. An orchestra of warbling and cooing played in my ear. There was an extraordinary sense of harmony between me and my inner self, and between the two of us and the world, everything being in its rightful place, without discord or distortion. In the whole world there was no single reason for speech or movement, for the universe moved in a rapture of ecstasy. This lasted but a short while. When I opened my eyes, consciousness struck at me like a policeman's fist, and I saw Wanas al-Damanhouri peering at me with concern. Only a few drowsy customers were left in the bar.

"You have slept deeply," said my companion. "You were obviously hungry for sleep."

I rested my heavy head in the palms of my hands. When I took them away in astonishment and looked down at them, I found that they glistened with drops of water.

"My head's wet," I protested.

"Yes, my friend tried to rouse you," he answered quietly.

"Somebody saw me in this state?"

"Don't worry, he is a good man. Have you not heard of Sheikh Zaabalawi?"

"Zaabalawi!" I exclaimed, jumping to my feet.

"Yes," he answered in surprise. "What's wrong?"

"Where is he?"

"I don't know where he is now. He was here and then he left."

I was about to run off in pursuit but found I was more exhausted than I had imagined. Collapsed over the table, I cried out in despair, "My sole reason for coming to you was to meet him! Help me to catch up with him or send someone after him."

The man called a vendor of prawns and asked him to seek out the sheikh and bring him back. Then he turned to me. "I didn't realize you were afflicted. I'm very sorry. . . ."

"You wouldn't let me speak," I said irritably.

"What a pity! He was sitting on this chair beside you the whole time. He was playing with a string of jasmine petals he had around his neck, a gift from one of his admirers, then, taking pity on you, he began to sprinkle some water on your head to bring you around."

"Does he meet you here every night?" I asked, my eyes not

leaving the doorway through which the vendor of prawns had left.

"He was with me tonight, last night, and the night before that, but before that I hadn't seen him for a month."

"Perhaps he will come tomorrow," I answered with a sigh.

"Perhaps."

"I am willing to give him any money he wants."

Wanas answered sympathetically, "The strange thing is that he is not open to such temptations, yet he will cure you if you meet him."

"Without charge?"

"Merely on sensing that you love him."

The vendor of prawns returned, having failed in his mission.

I recovered some of my energy and left the bar, albeit unsteadily. At every street corner I called out "Zaabalawi!" in the vague hope that I would be rewarded with an answering shout. The street boys turned contemptuous eyes on me till I sought refuge in the first available taxi.

The following evening I stayed up with Wanas al-Damanhouri till dawn, but the sheikh did not put in an appearance. Wanas informed me that he would be going away to the country and would not be returning to Cairo until he had sold the cotton crop.

I must wait, I told myself; I must train myself to be patient. Let me content myself with having made certain of the existence of Zaabalawi, and even of his affection for me, which encourages me to think that he will be prepared to cure me if a meeting takes place between us.

Sometimes, however, the long delay wearied me. I would become beset by despair and would try to persuade myself to dismiss him from my mind completely. How many weary people in this life know him not or regard him as a mere myth! Why, then, should I torture myself about him in this way?

No sooner, however, did my pains force themselves upon me than I would again begin to think about him, asking myself when I would be fortunate enough to meet him. The fact that I ceased to have any news of Wanas and was told he had gone to live abroad did not deflect me from my purpose; the truth of the matter was that I had become fully convinced that I had to find Zaabalawi.

Yes, I have to find Zaabalawi.

The Conjurer Made Off with the Dish

"The time has come for you to be useful," said my mother to me. And she slipped her hand into her pocket, saying, "Take this piaster and go off and buy some beans. Don't play on the way and keep away from the carts."

I took the dish, put on my clogs, and went out, humming a tune. Finding a crowd in front of the bean seller, I waited until I discovered a way through to the marble counter.

"A piaster's worth of beans, mister," I called out in my shrill voice.

He asked me impatiently, "Beans alone? With oil? With cooking butter?"

I did not answer, and he said roughly, "Make way for someone else."

I withdrew, overcome by embarrassment, and returned home defeated.

"Returning with the dish empty?" my mother shouted at me. "What did you do—spill the beans or lose the piaster, you naughty boy?"

"Beans alone? With oil? With cooking butter?—you didn't tell me," I protested.

"Stupid boy! What do you eat every morning?"

"I don't know."

"You good-for-nothing, ask him for beans with oil."

I went off to the man and said, "A piaster's worth of beans with oil, mister."

With a frown of impatience he asked, "Linseed oil? Vegetable oil? Olive oil?"

I was taken aback and again made no answer.

"Make way for someone else," he shouted at me.

I returned in a rage to my mother, who called out in astonishment, "You've come back empty-handed—no beans and no oil."

"Linseed oil? Vegetable oil? Olive oil? Why didn't you tell me?" I said angrily.

"Beans with oil means beans with linseed oil."

"How should I know?"

"You're a good-for-nothing, and he's a tiresome man—tell him beans with linseed oil."

I went off quickly and called out to the man while still some yards from his shop, "Beans with linseed oil, mister."

"Put the piaster on the counter," he said, plunging the ladle into the pot.

I put my hand into my pocket but did not find the piaster. I searched for it anxiously. I turned my pocket inside out but found no trace of it. The man withdrew the ladle empty, saying with disgust, "You've lost the piaster—you're not a boy to be depended on."

"I haven't lost it," I said, looking under my feet and round about me. "It was in my pocket all the time."

"Make way for someone else and stop bothering me."

I returned to my mother with an empty dish.

"Good grief, are you an idiot, boy?"

"The piaster . . ."

"What of it?"

"It's not in my pocket."

"Did you buy sweets with it?"

"I swear I didn't."

"How did you lose it?"

"I don't know."

"Do you swear by the Koran you didn't buy anything with it?"

"I swear."

"Is there a hole in your pocket?"

"No, there isn't."

"Maybe you gave it to the man the first time or the second."

"Maybe."

"Are you sure of nothing?"

"I'm hungry."

She clapped her hands together in a gesture of resignation.

"Never mind," she said. "I'll give you another piaster but I'll take it out of your money-box, and if you come back with an empty dish, I'll break your head."

I went off at a run, dreaming of a delicious breakfast. At the turning leading to the alleyway where the bean seller was, I saw a crowd of children and heard merry, festive sounds. My feet dragged as my heart was pulled toward them. At least let me have a fleeting glance. I slipped in among them and found the conjurer looking straight at me. A stupefying joy overwhelmed me; I was completely taken out of myself. With the whole of my being I became involved in the tricks of the rabbits and the eggs, and the snakes and the ropes. When the man came up to collect money, I drew back mumbling, "I haven't got any money."

He rushed at me savagely, and I escaped only with difficulty. I ran off, my back almost broken by his blow, and yet I was utterly happy as I made my way to the seller of beans.

"Beans with linseed oil for a piaster, mister," I said.

He went on looking at me without moving, so I repeated my request.

"Give me the dish," he demanded angrily.

The dish! Where was the dish? Had I dropped it while running? Had the conjurer made off with it?

"Boy, you're out of your mind!"

I retraced my steps, searching along the way for the lost dish. The place where the conjurer had been, I found empty, but the voices of children led me to him in a nearby lane. I moved around the circle. When the conjurer spotted me, he shouted out threateningly, "Pay up or you'd better scram."

"The dish!" I called out despairingly.

"What dish, you little devil?"

"Give me back the dish."

"Scram or I'll make you into food for snakes."

He had stolen the dish, yet fearfully I moved away out of sight and wept in grief. Whenever a passerby asked me why I was crying, I would reply, "The conjurer made off with the dish."

Through my misery I became aware of a voice saying, "Come along and watch!"

I looked behind me and saw a peep show had been set up. I saw dozens of children hurrying toward it and taking it in turns to stand in front of the peepholes, while the man began his tantalizing commentary to the pictures.

"There you've got the gallant knight and the most beautiful of all ladies, Zainat al-Banat."

My tears dried up, and I gazed in fascination at the box, completely forgetting the conjurer and the dish. Unable to overcome the temptation, I paid over the piaster and stood in front of the peephole next to a girl who was standing in front of the other one, and enchanting picture stories flowed across our vision. When I came back to my own world I realized I had lost both the piaster and the dish, and there was no sign of the conjurer. However, I gave no thought to the loss, so taken up was I with the pictures of chivalry, love, and deeds of daring. I forgot my hunger. I forgot even the fear of what threatened me at home. I took a few paces back so as to lean against the ancient wall of what had once been a treasury and the chief cadi's seat of office, and gave myself up wholly to my reveries. For a long while I dreamed of chivalry, of Zainat al-Banat and the ghoul. In my dream I spoke aloud, giving meaning to my words with gestures. Thrusting home the imaginary lance, I said, "Take that, O ghoul, right in the heart!"

"And he raised Zainat al-Banat up behind him on the horse," came back a gentle voice.

I looked to my right and saw the young girl who had been beside me at the performance. She was wearing a dirty dress and colored clogs and was playing with her long plait of hair. In her other hand were the red-and-white sweets called "lady's fleas," which she was leisurely sucking. We exchanged glances, and I lost my heart to her.

"Let's sit down and rest," I said to her.

She appeared to go along with my suggestion, so I took her by the arm and we went through the gateway of the ancient wall and sat down on a step of its stairway that went nowhere, a stairway that rose up until it ended in a platform behind which there could be seen the blue sky and minarets. We sat in silence, side by side. I pressed her hand, and we sat on in silence, not knowing what to say. I experienced feelings that were new, strange, and obscure. Putting my face close to hers, I breathed in the natural smell of her hair mingled with an odor of dust, and the fragrance of breath mixed with the aroma of sweets. I kissed her lips. I swallowed my saliva, which had taken on a sweetness from the dissolved "lady's fleas." I put my arm around her, without her uttering a word, kissing her cheek and lips. Her lips grew still as they received the kiss, then went back to sucking at the sweets. At last she decided to get up. I seized her arm anxiously. "Sit down," I said.

"I'm going," she replied simply.

"Where to?" I asked dejectedly.

"To the midwife Umm Ali," and she pointed to a house on the ground floor of which was a small ironing shop.

"Why?"

"To tell her to come quickly."

"Why?"

"My mother's crying in pain at home. She told me to go to the midwife Umm Ali and tell her to come along quickly."

"And you'll come back after that?"

She nodded her head in assent and went off. Her mentioning her mother reminded me of my own, and my heart missed a beat. Getting up from the ancient stairway, I made my way back home. I wept out loud, a tried method by which I would defend myself. I expected she would come to me, but she did not. I wandered from the kitchen to the bedroom but found no trace of her. Where had my mother gone? When would she return? I was fed up with being in the empty house. A good idea occurred to me. I took a dish from the kitchen and a piaster from my savings and went off immediately to the seller of beans. I found him asleep on a bench outside the shop, his face covered by his arm. The pots of beans had vanished and the long-necked bottles of oil had been put back on the shelf and the marble counter had been washed down.

"Mister," I whispered, approaching.

Hearing nothing but his snoring, I touched his shoulder. He raised his arm in alarm and looked at me through reddened eyes.

"Mister."

"What do you want?" he asked roughly, becoming aware of my presence and recognizing me.

"A piaster's worth of beans with linseed oil."

"Eh?"

"I've got the piaster and I've got the dish."

"You're crazy, boy," he shouted at me. "Get out or I'll bash your brains in."

When I did not move, he pushed me so violently I went sprawling onto my back. I got up painfully, struggling to hold back the crying that was twisting my lips. My hands were clenched, one on the dish and the other on the piaster. I threw him an angry look. I thought about returning home with my hopes dashed, but dreams of heroism and valor altered my plan of action. Resolutely I made a quick decision and with all my strength threw the dish at him. It flew through the air and struck him on the head, while I took to my heels, heedless of everything. I was convinced I had killed him, just as the knight had killed the ghoul. I did not stop running till I was near the ancient wall. Panting, I looked behind me but saw no signs of any pursuit. I stopped to get my breath, then asked myself what I should do now that the second dish was lost? Something warned me not to return home directly, and soon I had given myself over to a wave of indifference that bore me off where it willed. It meant a beating, neither more nor less, on my return, so let me put it off for a time. Here was the piaster in my hand, and I could have some sort of enjoyment with it before being punished. I decided to pretend I had forgotten I had done anything wrong—but where was the conjurer, where was the peep show? I looked everywhere for them to no avail.

Worn out by this fruitless searching, I went off to the ancient stairway to keep my appointment. I sat down to wait, imagining to myself the meeting. I yearned for another kiss redolent with the fragrance of sweets. I admitted to myself that the little girl had given me lovelier sensations than I had ever experienced. As I waited and dreamed, a whispering sound came from behind me. I climbed the stairs cautiously, and at the final landing I lay down flat on my face in order to see what was beyond, without anyone being able to notice me. I saw some ruins surrounded by a high wall, the last of what remained of the treasury and the chief cadi's seat of office. Directly under the stairs sat a man and a woman, and it was from them that the whispering came. The man looked like a tramp; the woman like one of those Gypsies that tend sheep. A suspicious inner voice told me that their meeting was similar to the one I had had. Their lips and the looks they exchanged spoke of this, but they showed astonishing expertise in the unimaginable things they did. My gaze became rooted upon them with curiosity, surprise, pleasure, and a certain amount of disquiet. At last they sat down side by side, neither of them taking any notice of the other. After quite a while the man said, "The money!"

"You're never satisfied," she said irritably.

Spitting on the ground, he said, "You're crazy."

"You're a thief."

He slapped her hard with the back of his hand, and she gathered up a handful of earth and threw it in his face. Then, his face soiled with dirt, he sprang at her, fastening his fingers on her windpipe, and a bitter fight ensued. In vain she gathered all her strength to escape from his grip. Her voice failed her, her eyes bulged out of their sockets, while her feet struck out at the air. In dumb terror, I stared at the scene till I saw a thread of blood trickling down from her nose. A scream escaped from my mouth. Before the man raised his head, I had crawled backward. Descending the stairs at a jump, I raced off like mad to wherever my legs might carry me. I did not stop running till I was breathless. Gasping for breath, I was quite unaware of my surroundings, but when I came to myself I found I was under a raised vault at the middle of a crossroads. I had never set foot there before and had no idea of where I was in relation to our quarter. On both sides sat sightless beggars, and crossing from all directions were people who paid attention to no one. In terror I realized I had lost my way and that countless difficulties lay in wait for me before I found my way home. Should I resort to asking one of the passersby to direct me? What, though, would happen if chance should lead me to a man like the seller of beans or the tramp of the waste plot? Would a miracle come about whereby I would see my mother approaching so that I could eagerly hurry toward her? Should I try to make my own way, wandering about till I came across some familiar landmark that would indicate the direction I should take?

I told myself that I should be resolute and make a quick decision. The day was passing, and soon mysterious darkness would descend.

The Answer Is No

The important piece of news that the new headmaster had arrived spread through the school. She heard of it in the women teachers' common room as she was casting a final glance at the day's lessons. There was no getting away from joining the other teachers in congratulating him, and from shaking him by the hand too. A shudder passed through her body, but it was unavoidable.

"They speak highly of his ability," said a colleague of hers. "And they talk too of his strictness."

It had always been a possibility that might occur, and now it had. Her pretty face paled, and a staring look came to her wide black eyes.

When the time came, the teachers went in single file, decorously attired, to his open room. He stood behind his desk as he received the men and women. He was of medium height, with a tendency to portliness, and had a spherical face, hooked nose, and bulging eyes; the first thing that could be seen of him was a thick, puffed-up mustache, arched like a foam-laden wave. She advanced with her eyes fixed on his chest. Avoiding his gaze, she stretched out her hand. What was she to say? Just what the others had said? However, she kept silent, uttered not a word. What, she wondered, did his eyes express? His rough hand shook hers, and he said in a gruff voice, "Thanks." She turned elegantly and moved off.

She forgot her worries through her daily tasks, though she did not look in good shape. Several of the girls remarked, "Miss is in a bad mood." When she returned to her home at the beginning of the Pyramids Road, she changed her clothes and sat down to eat with her mother. "Everything all right?" inquired her mother, looking her in the face.

"Badran, Badran Badawi," she said briefly. "Do you remember him? He's been appointed our headmaster."

"Really!"

Then, after a moment of silence, she said, "It's of no importance at all—it's an old and long-forgotten story."

After eating, she took herself off to her study to rest for a while before correcting some exercise books. She had forgotten him completely. No, not completely. How could he be forgotten completely? When he had first come to give her a private lesson in mathematics, she was fourteen years of age. In fact not quite fourteen. He had been twenty-five years older, the same age as her father. She had said to her mother, "His appearance is a mess, but he explains things well." And her mother had said, "We're not concerned with what he looks like; what's important is how he explains things."

He was an amusing person, and she got on well with him and benefited from his knowledge. How, then, had it happened? In her innocence she had not noticed any change in his behavior to put her on her guard. Then one day he had been left on his own with her, her father having gone to her aunt's clinic. She had not the slightest doubts about a man she regarded as a second father. How, then, had it happened? Without love or desire on her part the thing had happened. She had asked in terror about what had occurred, and he had told her, "Don't be frightened or sad. Keep it to yourself and I'll come and propose to you the day you come of age."

And he had kept his promise and had come to ask for her hand. By then she had attained a degree of maturity that gave her an understanding of the dimensions of her tragic position. She had found that she had no love or respect for him and that he was as far as he could be from her dreams and from the ideas she had formed of what constituted an ideal and moral person. But what was to be done? Her father had passed away two years ago, and her mother had been taken aback by the forwardness of the man. However, she had said to her, "I know your attachment to your personal independence, so I leave the decision to you."

She had been conscious of the critical position she was in. She had either to accept or to close the door forever. It was the sort of situation that could force her into something she detested. She was the rich, beautiful girl, a byword in Abbasiyya for her nobility of character, and now here she was struggling helplessly in a well-sprung trap, while he looked down at her with rapacious eyes. Just as she had hated his strength, so too did she hate her own weakness. To have abused her innocence was one thing, but for him to have the upper hand now that she was fully in possession of her faculties was something else. He had said, "So here I am, making good my promise because I love you." He had also said, "I know of your love of teaching, and you will complete your studies at the College of Science."

She had felt such anger as she had never felt before. She had rejected coercion in the same way as she rejected ugliness. It had meant little to her to sacrifice marriage. She had welcomed being on her own, for solitude accompanied by self-respect was not loneliness. She had also guessed he was after her money. She had told her mother quite straightforwardly, "No," to which her mother had replied, "I am astonished you did not make this decision from the first moment."

The man had blocked her way outside and said, "How can you refuse? Don't you realize the outcome?" And she had replied with an asperity he had not expected, "For me any outcome is preferable to being married to you."

After finishing her studies, she had wanted something to do

to fill her spare time, so she had worked as a teacher. Chances to marry had come time after time, but she had turned her back on them all.

"Does no one please you?" her mother asked her.

"I know what I'm doing," she had said gently.

"But time is going by."

"Let it go as it pleases, I am content."

Day by day she becomes older. She avoids love, fears it. With all her strength she hopes that life will pass calmly, peacefully, rather than happily. She goes on persuading herself that happiness is not confined to love and motherhood. Never has she regretted her firm decision. Who knows what the morrow holds? But she was certainly unhappy that he should again make his appearance in her life, that she would be dealing with him day after day, and that he would be making of the past a living and painful present.

Then, the first time he was alone with her in his room, he asked her, "How are you?"

She answered coldly, "I'm fine."

He hesitated slightly before inquiring, "Have you not . . . I mean, did you get married?"

In the tone of someone intent on cutting short a conversation, she said, "I told you, I'm fine."

The Time and the Place

It happened on my last night in the old house, or rather on the night that it had been agreed was to be the last. Despite being old and clearly out of place in a contemporary setting, the house possessed a character of its own. It had become, as it were, an ancient monument, and this was further accentuated by a location that gave one a view of a square born the same year as the city of Cairo itself. By virtue of having inherited the house, we had been brought up there. Then, by reason of the discord of different generations, a feeling of antipathy had grown up between us and the house, and we found ourselves aspiring to the bright new milieux, far distant from the stone walls that lay embedded in narrow alleyways.

I was sitting in the spacious living room, on a dilapidated couch, which it had been decided to dispose of, under a skylight firmly closed against the caprices of the autumn weather. I was sipping at a glass of cinnamon tea and gazing at a small brass ewer standing on a table in front of me; out of it protruded a stick of Javanese incense, slowly giving out a thread of fragrant smoke that coiled and curled under the lamplight in the silence of leave-taking. For no reason a listlessness gripped at my feeling of well-being, after which I was overcome by a mysterious sense of unease. I steeled myself to fight against it, but the whole of life piled up before my eyes in a fleeting flash, like a ball of light flung forward with cosmic speed; in no time it was extinguished, giving itself up to the unknown, submerged in its endless depths.

I told myself that I was acquainted with such tricks and that the departure tomorrow, so arbitrarily fixed, was reminding me of one's final departure, when the cameleer raises his voice to intone the very last song. I began to seek distraction from the sorrows of leave-taking by imagining the new abode in the wide street under the densely growing branches of mimosa lebbek trees, and the new life that gave promise of immeasurable sophisticated delights. No sooner had the cinnamon tea come to rest inside me than I made a sudden and gigantic leap that transferred me from one actuality into another. From deep within me rose a call that with boundless confidence invited me to open doors, to pull aside the screen, to invade space, and grab hold of approval and forgiveness from the atmosphere so fragrant with incense. Cares, anxieties, and thoughts of annihilation all faded away, drowned in a flood of energy and a sense of enchantment and ecstasy, and my heart quivered in a wonderful dance brought into being by passionate exuberance.

Within me flashed a light, which assumed the form of a person. Presenting me with a glass of wine filled to overflowing, he said to me amiably, "Accept the gift of a miracle." I expected something to happen and it did: dissolving into nothingness, the living room was replaced by a vast courtyard that extended far into the distance until it met its boundary with the square in a thick white wall. The courtyard was covered with grassy rounds and crescents, with a well in the middle. At a short distance from the well was a lofty palm tree. I found myself wavering between two sensations: a feeling that told me I was witnessing a scene I had never viewed before, and another that told me that there was nothing strange about it, that I had both seen it and was remembering it. I made a violent movement with my head so as to bring myself back to the present, if in fact my mind had been wandering. The scene merely became clearer, more dominating, while between the palm tree and the well a human being took shape. This person, though concealed within a black gibba and a tall green turban, was none other than myself; despite the flowing beard, the face was mine. Once again, I moved my head, but the scene merely became even clearer and sharper; the tawny light indicated that the sun was setting. There also took shape, between the well and the date palm, a middle-aged man who was dressed similarly to myself. I saw him handing me a small box and saying, "These are days of insecurity. You must hide it under the ground until you return to it in due time."

"Wouldn't it be best," I asked him, "for me to have a look at it before hiding it?"

"No, no," he said firmly, "that would cause you to be hasty in taking action before a year is up, and you would perish."

"Have I to wait a year?"

"At least, then follow that which it enjoins." He was silent for a while, then he continued. "These are days of insecurity," he cautioned, "and your house is liable to be searched. You must therefore hide it deep down." And the two of them set about digging close by the date palm. Having buried the box, they heaped earth on top of it and carefully leveled the surface. Then the middle-aged man said, "I'll leave you in the care of the Almighty. Be cautious—these are days of insecurity."

At this the scene vanished as though it had never been. The living room of the old house returned, and there was still some of the stick of incense left. Quickly I started to awaken from my state of elation and to revert to reality in all its material solidity, though for a long time I was in a state of agitated excitement. Could it have been a figment of the imagination? This was the obvious explanation, but how could I accept that and forget the scene that had assumed such concrete form, a scene that in all its dimensions had exuded such verisimilitude? I had lived some past reality that was no less solid than the reality of the present, and had seen myself—or one of my forebears—and part of an era that had passed away. It was not possible for me to doubt that without doubting my mind and senses. Naturally, I did not know how it had come about, but I knew for a fact that it had. One question forced itself upon me: Why had it happened? And why had it happened on this, my last night in the old house? All at once I felt that I was being required to do something, something from which there was no escape.

Could it be that "the other one" had taken out the box after the expiration of a year and had done that which he was directed to do? Had he reached the end of his patience and, acting too hastily, perished? Had his plan turned against him in those days of insecurity? How unrelentingly insistent was the desire to know! A strange thought occurred to me, which was that the past had been manifested to me only because "the other one" had been prevented from getting at the box and that I was being called upon to dig it up and to put into effect what was directed should be done, after it had been unknown, overlooked for such a long period of time. It was ordering me not to leave the old house so that I might act on some ancient command, the time for whose implementation had not yet arrived. Despite the fact that the whole situation was garbed in a wrapping woven of dreams, and wholly at odds with reason, it nonetheless took control of me with a despotic force. My heart became filled with the delights and pains of living in expectation.

That whole night I did not sleep a single moment, as my imagination went roaming through the vastness of time that comprised past, present, and future together, drunk with the intoxication that total freedom brings. The idea of departure was out of the question. I was overwhelmed by the desire to excavate the unknown past in the hope of coming across the word of command that had so long lain dormant. Then I pondered what should be done next. By comparing the scene that had passed away with the one that lay before me, I calculated that the old site of the date palm was where the small stairway led up to the living room. Digging, therefore, must start at a short distance from it, adjacent to the living room window.

I was then faced with the difficulty of informing my brother and sister that I had changed my mind about leaving, after having agreed with them to do so. We were still at university; I was in my last year at the Faculty of Law, while my brother, a year my junior, was studying engineering, and my sister, two years younger than I, was studying medicine. Both of them protested at my sudden change of mind, finding none of my reasons convincing, while at the same time insisting on making the move on their own and expressing the hope that I would soon join them. Before leaving, they reminded me that we had agreed to put the house up for sale so as to profit from the rise in property prices, and I raised no objection. Thus we separated for the first time in our lives, having thought that only marriage or death would ever come between us.

Nothing remained but to start work. I was in truth frightened of the possibility that it would reveal nothing, but I was driven by a force that would not let me turn back, and I made up my mind to dig on my own at night in utter secrecy. I went to work with an axe, a shovel, a basket, and tireless zeal, and soon I was stained with dust and my lungs were filled with it. There lodged in my nostrils a smell full of the nostalgia of bygone days. I continued till I had dug down to a depth of my own height, helped by nothing but a feeling that I was drawing near to the truth. Then a blow from the axe gave back an unfamiliar sound that bespoke the presence of an unfamiliar substance. My heart beat so wildly that I found myself trembling all over. In the candlelight I saw the box staring up at me with a face dusty yet alive, as though reproaching me for my long delay, rebuking me for the loss of those many years, and making plain its displeasure at having kept imprisoned a word that should have been made known. At the same time I was being presented with a truth in a concrete form that was undeniable, an embodied miracle, a victory scored against time.

I brought the box up to the surface, then hurried off to the living room, carrying with me the evidence that had ferried me across from a state of dreaming to that of reality and had made a mockery of all accepted concepts. I brushed away the dust, opened the box, and found inside a letter folded up in a wrapping of ragged linen. I spread it out carefully and proceeded to read.

O my son, may God Almighty protect you.

The year has gone by and each has come to know his path.

Leave not your house for it is the most beautiful in Cairo, besides which, the Believers know no other house, no other safe refuge.

The time has come for you to meet the Guardian of the Sanctuary, our Master Arif al-Baqallani, so go to his house, which is the third one to the right as you enter Aram Gour Alley, and mention to him the password, which is: If I am absent He appears, and if He appears He will cause me to be absent.

Thus will you discharge your duty, and fortune will smile upon you, and you will obtain that which the Believers wish for you, also that which you wish for yourself.

I read the letter so many times that the reading became mechanical and meaningless. As for my old associate, I had no knowledge as to what his fate had been. I was nevertheless certain that the house was no longer the most beautiful in Cairo, nor a safe refuge for the Believers, and that Arif al-Baqallani, Guardian of the Sanctuary, no longer existed. Wherefore, then, the vision? And wherefore the labor? Was it possible that a miracle of such magnitude could occur for no reason? Was it not conceivable that it was demanding that I go to the third house in Aram Gour Alley so that something might be bestowed upon me that I had not foreseen? Did I have it in me to stop myself from going there, drawn as I was by an avid curiosity and a longing that rejected the idea of my unique miracle ending in a futile jest? Under cover of night I set off, several hundred years late for my appointment. I found the alley lying supine under a darkness from whose depths showed the glimmer of a lamp. Except for a few individuals who quickly crossed to the main road, I saw no sign of human life. I passed by the first house and reached the second. At the third I came to a stop. I turned toward it like someone walking in a dream. I perceived that it possessed a small courtyard lying behind a low wall and that there were indistinct human forms. Before I was able to back away, the door was opened and two tall men in European dress came out. With a quickly executed flanking movement, they barred my path. Then one of them said, "Go inside and meet the person you've come to meet."

Taken by surprise, I said, "I didn't come to meet anyone, but I'd be glad to know the name of the person living in the house."

"Really! And why?"

Pushing aside a feeling of apprehension, I said, "I'd like to know if the person living here is from the al-Baqallani family."

"Enough of al-Baqallani—just continue your journey to its end."

It occurred to me that the two of them were security men, and I was seized with alarm and confusion. "There's no journey, no meeting," I said.

"You'll change your mind."

Each seized me by an arm, and despite my struggles, herded

me inside. Torn from a dream, I was thrust into a nightmare. I was taken into a lighted reception room in the center of which stood a person in a white galabeya, handcuffed. Round about the room I saw several men of the same type as the two who had herded me inside. One of the two men said, "He was coming to meet his friend."

A man—I guessed him to be the leader of the group—turned to the man under arrest. "One of your comrades?" he asked him.

"I've not seen him before," answered the young man sullenly.

Looking toward me, the leader asked, "Are you going to repeat the same story, or will you save yourself and us the trouble and confess?"

"I swear by Almighty God," I exclaimed vehemently, "that I have no connection with anything you may suspect."

He stretched out his hand. "Your identity card." I gave him the card. He read it, then asked me, "What brought you here?"

I pointed to the two men and said in an aggrieved tone, "They brought me here by force."

"They hunted you out from off the streets?"

"I came to the alley to ask about the al-Baqallani family."

"And what should cause you to ask about them?"

Utterly confused, I was conscious of the wariness inevitably felt by anyone under questioning. "I read about them in a history," I said, "I read that they used to live in the third house to the right as you enter this alley."

"Tell me of the work in which you read that."

I became even more confused and made no answer.

"Lying won't do any good, in fact it'll do you more harm."

"What do you want of me?" I asked in near despair.

"We're taking you in for questioning," he said quietly.

"You won't believe me if I tell you the truth," I shouted.

"What might this truth be?"

I gave a sigh; there was dust in my spittle. Then I started to talk. "I was sitting alone in the living room of my house . . ." And I divulged my secret under their stern and derisive gazes. When I had finished, the man said coldly, "Pretending to be mad also won't do any good."

Taking the letter from my pocket, I called out joyfully, "Here's the proof for you."

He scrutinized it, then muttered to himself, "A strange piece of paper whose secret we shall shortly discover." He began carefully reading the lines of writing, and his lips parted in a scornful smile. "An obvious code," he mumbled. Then he looked toward the owner of the house, who was under arrest, and asked him, "Would you be Arif al-Baqallani? Is that your code name?"

"I have no code name," said the young man contemptuously, "and this stranger is nothing but one of your stooges you've brought along so as to trump up a charge against me, but I'm well aware of such tricks."

"Wouldn't it be best," one of the assistants inquired of the leader, "to stay on in case some others turn up and fall into the trap?"

"We'll wait until dawn," said the leader, and he gestured to the two men holding me, at which, disregarding my protests, they began putting handcuffs on me. I could not believe how things had turned out. How could they begin with a wonderful miracle and end up with such a reversal of fortune? I neither believed it could be nor gave way to despair. I was for certain up to my ears in trouble, yet the vision had not been revealed to me for mere jest. I must admit my childish error, I must reconsider things, I must put trust in time.

A heavy silence enclosed us. I brought to mind my brother and sister in the new house, and the gaping hole in the old. The situation presented itself to me from the point of view of someone standing outside it and I could not help but give a laugh. But no one turned to me, no one broke the silence.

Blessed Night

It was nothing but a single room in the unpretentious Nouri Alley, off Clot Bey Street. In the middle of the room was the bar and the shelf embellished with bottles. It was called The Flower and was passionately patronized by old men addicted to drink. Its barman was advanced in years, excessively quiet, a man who inspired silence and yet effused a cordial friendliness. Unlike other taverns, The Flower dozed in a delightful tranquility. The regulars would converse inwardly, with glances rather than words. On the night that was blessed, the barman departed from his traditional silence.

"Yesterday," he said, "I dreamed that a gift would be presented to a man of good fortune. . . ."

Safwan's heart broke into a song with gentle lute accompaniment, while alcoholic waves flowed through him like electricity as he congratulated himself with the words "O blessed, blessed night!" He left the bar, reeling drunk, and plunged into the sublime night under an autumn sky that was not without a twinkling of stars. He made his way toward Nuzha Street, cutting across the square, glowing with an intoxication unadulterated by the least sensation of drowsiness. The street was humbled under the veil of darkness, except for the light from the regularly spaced streetlamps, the shops having closed their doors and given themselves up to sleep. He stood in front of his house: the fourth on the right, Number 42, a single-storied house fronted by an old courtyard of whose garden nothing remained but a solitary towering date palm. Astonished at the dense darkness that surrounded the house, he wondered why his wife had not as usual turned on the light by the front door. It seemed that the house was manifesting itself in a new, gloomily forlorn shape and that it exuded a smell like that of old age. Raising his voice, he called out. "Hey there!"

From behind the fence there rose before his eyes the form of a man, who coughed and inquired, "Who are you? What do you want?"

Safwan was startled at the presence of this stranger and asked sharply, "And who are you? What's brought you to my house?"

"Your house?" said the man in a hoarse, angry voice.

"Who are you?"

"I am the guardian for religious endowment properties."

"But this is my house."

"This house has been deserted for ages," the man scoffed. "People avoid it because it's rumored to be haunted by spirits."

Safwan decided he must have lost his way, and hurried back toward the square. He gave it a long comprehensive look, then raised his head to the street sign and read out loud, "Nuzha." So again he entered the street and counted off the houses until he arrived at the fourth. There he stood in a state of bewilderment, almost of panic: he could find neither his own house nor the haunted one. Instead he saw an empty space, a stretch of wasteland lying between the other houses. "Is it my house that I've lost or my mind?" he wondered.

He saw a policeman approaching, examining the locks of the shops. He stood in his path and pointed toward the empty wasteland. "What do you see there?"

The policeman stared at him suspiciously and muttered, "As you can see, it's a piece of wasteland where they sometimes set up funeral pavilions."

"That's just where I should have found my house," said Safwan. "I left it there with my wife inside it in the pink of health only this afternoon, so when could it have been pulled down and all the rubble cleared away?"

The policeman concealed an involuntary smile behind a stern official glare and said brusquely, "Ask that deadly poison in your stomach!"

"You are addressing a former general manager," said Safwan haughtily. At this the policeman grasped him by the arm and led him off. "Drunk and disorderly in the public highway!"

He took Safwan to the Daher police station, a short distance away, where he was brought before the officer on a charge of being drunk and disorderly. The officer took pity on him, however, because of his age and his respectable appearance. "Your identity card?"

Safwan produced it and said, "I'm quite in my right mind, it's just that there's no trace of my house."

"Well, now there's a new type of theft!" said the officer, laughing. "I really don't believe it!"

"But I'm speaking the truth," said Safwan in alarm.

"The truth's being unfairly treated, but I'll be lenient in deference to your age." Then he said to the policeman, "Take him to Number 42 Nuzha Street."

Accompanied by the policeman, Safwan finally found himself in front of his house as he knew it. Despite his drunken state he was overcome with confusion. He opened the outer door, crossed the courtyard, and put on the light at the entrance, where he was immediately taken aback, for he found himself in an entrance he had never before set eyes on. There was absolutely no connection between it and the entrance of the house in which he had lived for about half a century, and whose furniture and walls were all in a state of decay. He decided to retreat before his mistake was revealed, so he darted into the street, where he stood scrutinizing the house from the outside.

It was his house all right, from the point of view of its features and site, and he had opened the door with his own key, no doubt about it. What, then, had changed the inside? He had seen a small chandelier, and the walls had been papered. There was also a new carpet. In a way it was his house, and in another way it was not. And what about his wife, Sadriyya? "I've been drinking for half a century," he said aloud, "so what is it about this blessed night?"

He imagined his seven married daughters looking at him with tearful eyes. He determined, though, to solve the problem by himself, without recourse to the authorities—which would certainly mean exposing himself to the wrath of the law. Going up to the fence, he began clapping his hands, at which the front door was opened by someone whose features he could not make out. A woman's voice could be heard asking, "What's keeping you outside?"

It seemed, though he could not be certain, that it was the voice of a stranger. "Whose house is this, please?" he inquired.

"Are you that drunk? It's just too much!"

"I'm Safwan," he said cautiously.

"Come in or you'll wake the people sleeping."

"Are you Sadriyya?"

"Heaven help us! There's someone waiting for you inside."

"At this hour?"

"He's been waiting since ten."

"Waiting for me?"

She mumbled loudly in exasperation, and he inquired again, "Are you Sadriyya?"

Her patience at an end, she shouted, "Heaven help us!"

He advanced, at first stealthily, then without caring, and found himself in the new entrance. He saw that the door of the sitting room was open, with the lights brightly illuminating the interior. As for the woman, she had disappeared. He entered the sitting room, which revealed itself to him in a new garb, as the entrance had. Where had the old room with its ancient furniture gone to? Walls recently painted and a large chandelier from which Spanish-style lamps hung, a blue carpet, a spacious sofa and armchairs: it was a splendid room. In the foreground sat a man he had not seen before: thin, of a dark brown complexion, with a nose reminding one of a parrot's beak, and a certain impetuosity in the eyes. He was wearing a black suit, although autumn was only just coming in. The man addressed him irritably. "How late you are for our appointment!"

Safwan was both taken aback and angry. "What appointment? Who are you?"

"That's just what I expected—you'd forgotten!" the man exclaimed. "It's the same old complaint repeated every single day, whether it's the truth or not. It's no use, it's out of the question. . . ."

"What is this raving nonsense?" Safwan shouted in exasperation.

Restraining himself, the man said, "I know you're a man who enjoys his drink and sometimes overdoes it."

"You're speaking to me as though you were in charge of me, while I don't even know you. I'm amazed you should impose your presence on a house in the absence of its owner."

He gave a chilly smile. "Its owner?"

"As though you doubt it!" Safwan said vehemently. "I see I'll have to call the police."

"So they can arrest you for being drunk and disorderly—and for fraud?"

"Shut up—you insolent imposter!"

The man struck one palm against the other and said, "You're pretending not to know who I am so as to escape from your commitments. It's out of the question . . ."

"I don't know you and I don't know what you're talking about."

"Really? Are you alleging you forgot and are therefore innocent? Didn't you agree to sell your house and wife and fix tonight for completing the final formalities?"

Safwan, in a daze, exclaimed, "What a lying devil you are!"

"As usual. You're all the same—shame on you!" said the other, with a shrug of the shoulders.

"You're clearly mad."

"I have the proof and witnesses."

"I've never heard of anyone having done such a thing before."

"But it happens every moment. You're putting on a good act, even though you're drunk."

In extreme agitation, Safwan said, "I demand you leave at once."

"No, let's conclude the incompleted formalities," said the other in a voice full of confidence.

He got up and went toward the closed door that led to the interior of the house. He rapped on it, then returned to his seat. Immediately there entered a short man with a pug nose and prominent forehead, carrying under his arm a file stuffed with papers. He bowed in greeting and sat down. Safwan directed a venomous glare at him and exclaimed, "Since when has my house become a shelter for the homeless?"

The first man, introducing the person who had just entered, said, "The lawyer."

At which Safwan asked him brusquely, "And who gave you permission to enter my house?"

"You're in a bad way," said the lawyer, smiling, "but may God forgive you. What are you so angry about?"

"What insolence!"

Without paying any attention to what Safwan had said, the lawyer went on. "The deal is undoubtedly to your advantage."

"What deal?" asked Safwan in bewilderment.

"You know exactly what I mean, and I would like to tell you that it's useless your thinking of going back on it now. The law is on our side, and common sense too. Let me ask you: Do you consider this house to be really yours?"

For the first time Safwan felt at a loss. "Yes and no," he said.

"Was it in this condition when you left it?"

"Not at all."

"Then it's another house?"

"Yet it's the same site, number, and street."

"Ah, those are fortuitous incidentals that don't affect the essential fact—and there's something else."

He got up, rapped on the door, and returned to his seat. All at once a beautiful middle-aged woman, well dressed and with a mournful mien, entered and seated herself alongside the first man. The lawyer resumed his questioning. "Do you recognize in this lady your wife?"

It seemed to Safwan that she did possess a certain similarity, but he could not stop himself from saying, "Not at all."

"Fine—the house is neither your house, nor the lady your wife. Thus nothing remains but for you to sign the final agreement and then you can be off. . . ."

"Off! Where to?"

"My dear sir, don't be stubborn. The deal is wholly to your advantage, and you know it."

The telephone rang, although it was very late at night. The caller was the barman. Safwan was astonished that the man should be telephoning him for the first time in his life. "Safwan Bey," he said, "Sign without delay."

"But do you know. . . ."

"Sign. It's the chance of a lifetime."

The receiver was replaced at the other end. Safwan considered the short conversation and found himself relaxing. In a second his state of mind changed utterly, his face took on a cheerful expression, and a sensation of calm spread throughout his body. The feeling of tension left him, and he signed. When he had done so, the lawyer handed him a small but somewhat heavy suitcase and said, "May the Almighty bless your comings and goings. In this suitcase is all that a happy man needs in this world."

The first man clapped, and there entered an extremely portly man, with a wide smile and a charming manner. Introducing him to Safwan, the lawyer said, "This is a trustworthy man and an expert at his work. He will take you to your new abode. It is truly a profitable deal."

The portly man made his way outside, and Safwan followed him, quiet and calm, his hand gripping the handle of the suitcase. The man walked ahead of him into the night, and Safwan followed. Affected by the fresh air, he staggered and realized that he had not recovered from the intoxication of the blessed night. The man quickened his pace, and the distance between them grew, so Safwan in turn, despite his drunken state, walked faster, his gaze directed toward the specter of the other man, while wondering how it was that he combined such agility with portliness. "Take it easy, sir!" Safwan called out to him.

But it was as though he had spurred the man on to greater speed, for he broke into strides so rapid that Safwan was forced to hurl himself forward for fear he would lose him, and thus lose his last hope. Frightened he would be incapable of keeping up the pace, he once again called out to the man. "Take it easy or I'll get lost!"

At this the other, unconcerned about Safwan, began to run. Safwan, in terror, raced ahead, heedless of the consequences. This caused him great distress, but all to no avail, for the man plunged into the darkness and disappeared from sight. Safwan was frightened the man would arrive ahead of him at Yanabi Square, where various roads split up, and he would not know which one the man had taken. He therefore began running as fast as possible, determined to catch up.

His efforts paid off, for once again he caught a glimpse of the specter of the man at the crossroads. He saw him darting forward toward the fields, ignoring the branch roads that turned off to the eastern and western parts of the city. Safwan hurried along behind him and continued running without stopping, and without the least feeling of weakness. His nostrils were filled with delightful aromas that stirred up all kinds of sensations he had never before properly experienced and enjoyed.

When the two of them were alone in the vast void of earth and sky, the portly man gradually began to slow down until he had reverted to a mere brisk trot, then to a walk. Finally he stopped, and Safwan caught up with him and also came to a breathless stop. He looked around at the all-pervading darkness, with the glittering lights of faint stars. "Where's the new abode?" he asked.

The man maintained his silence. At the same time, Safwan began to feel the incursion of a new weight bearing down upon his shoulders and his whole body. The weight grew heavier and heavier and then rose upward to his head. It seemed to him that his feet would plunge deep into the ground. The pressure became so great that he could no longer bear it and, with a sudden spontaneous burst of energy, he took off his shoes. Then, the pressure working its way upward, he stripped himself of his jacket and trousers and flung them to the ground. This made no real difference, so he rid himself of his underclothes, heedless of the dampness of autumn. He was ablaze with pain and, groaning, he abandoned the suitcase on the ground. At that moment it seemed to him that he had regained his balance, that he was capable of taking the few steps that still remained. He waited for his companion to do something, but the man was sunk in silence. Safwan wanted to converse with him, but talk was impossible, and the overwhelming silence slipped through the pores of his skin to his very heart. It seemed that in a little while he would be hearing the conversation that was passing between the stars.

The Ditch

Despite the great care I take in respect to personal hygiene and health in general, the sensation of dirt and disease besets me like some constant nagging thought.

I do not dwell solely in a human body, but also in an ancient and dilapidated flat in a decrepit alley submerged in garbage. The ceiling of the flat is bare of paint and reveals in places colorless veins, the walls are split into parallel and intersecting lines, while the floor has burst out into bulges and cavities that are in constant strife, through threadbare rugs, with the soles of one's feet. In summer the ceiling and walls exude a scorching heat, in winter a damp drizzle. The stairs are being eaten away, and one of the steps has come apart, so that half of it has collapsed, presenting an obstacle to anyone going up or down, and a not inconsiderable danger in the dark. On top of all this there is the crack that runs down the outside of the house on the side that abuts the lavatories, a side where the mortar and lime have flaked off and the stones have become exposed.

Hosni Alley is now without a sidewalk altogether, and no one recollects that it used to have two—no one, that is, other than myself, since I was actually born in the house. In this I am unlike the families of Ibrahim Effendi, the occupier of the middle floor, and of Sheikh Moharram, the tenant on the ground floor, who came to the house at the very earliest twenty years ago.

In my childhood days, the house was of mature age and in fair shape, and the alley, paved with stones and with two sidewalks, was no less splendid than Shurafa Street, to which it sloped down. The two sidewalks have by now disappeared under dirt and garbage, which, accumulating day by day, advances from the two sides toward the middle of the narrow road. Soon all that will be left will be a ditchlike passageway by which to come and go; it may even become so narrow as not to admit the body of Sitt Fawziyya, the wife of Ibrahim Effendi.

The shadow of times long past, the expectation of the house collapsing, and the diffusion of filth all pervaded my feelings and gave me a sensation of disease—and of fear as well. I was alone in a flat whose earlier occupants had been dispersed among new houses and the cemeteries. In addition, I was a civil servant, the one and only civil servant in a house that was well on its way to falling down, a civil servant groaning in the grip of rising prices and asking himself what would be his fate were an earthquake to occur or—in these days ominous with the possibilities of war—an air raid. Or what would happen were the house to bring to a close its exhausted life and die a natural death. Then I would make up my mind to chase away these anxieties with the same intensity as they were chasing me, and to commit myself to God's care and not to anticipate trouble before it actually came. At the café among my friends (overworked civil servants), or in front of the café television, I would become oblivious of my worries. But they would return in their most concentrated form on the first day of every month. This was a day about which both Sheikh Moharram and Sitt Fawziyya (who because of her strong personality used to act for her husband in all business matters) were extremely anxious, while I too would be full of apprehension. It was on that day that Abd al-Fattah Effendi, a postman and owner of the old house, would show up.

A man in his fifties, he still persisted in wearing a tarboosh; he was an unattractive person, though not perhaps because of any particular defect. I would become aware of his presence when I heard Sitt Fawziyya chiding him harshly, not letting him get a word in edgeways. As for me, It would deal with him with all the tact of which I was capable. I would receive him and sit him down on the only sofa and give him tea. He used to enjoy returning my greeting by saying, "I'd like someday to come and find you'd done your religious duty by getting married."

Concealing the fact that I had a lump in my throat, I would ask him, "Have you got a bride and a wedding going for free?"

He would blow at the steam from thc tea, take a noisy sip, and nod his head without uttering a word. I would hand the rent to him—three pounds—and he would take it, smiling scornfully, and saying, as he counted the money off between his fingers, "Less than the price of a kilo of meat—and they call me a landlord!" Then, encouraged by my silence, he would continue, "It's money that's destined for orphans, I swear by God."

And I'd say, "Two wretches squabbling over nothing—but what's to be done?"

"If you weren't occupying the house, I'd have sold it for a good amount." Then, in an admonitory tone, "It's on the way to collapsing. Didn't the Council warn you?"

"And are we to throw ourselves into the street?" I would inquire.

I am always deprived of the feeling of stability and security, as well as of being clean and healthy. Even so, I am better off than others, for I am at least on my own—from lack of means rather than from choice, but I am nevertheless on my own: a lonely and repressed hermit in a house about to fall down in an alley buried under garbage. I perform miracles to obtain a tasty meal (though not all that often) and a suit of clothes to cover the self-respect of a branch office manager. I dream of a home like those I see in the advertisements of the cooperatives and a bride like those on view in the weekly "brides" page—or even like Sitt Fawziyya. I console myself by reading *The Finery of the Saints*, the lives of pious, ascetic saints who live trusting in God, casting worldly cares aside, and finding refuge in everlasting peace. However, some chance item of news about a house collapsing, or about the police forcibly evacuating a building immediately after one side of it has come apart, would shake me to the core. Such news would call me back from the paradise of the saints and fill me with terror. Where would the people go? What belongings would be left to them? How would they manage? My sense of loneliness would be redoubled, despite the fact that the family I belonged to was a veritable tribe, scattered over different parts of the city, brothers and sisters and other relatives. And yet, with all that, what a suffocating loneliness! There were kind enough feelings about, but not a house to welcome a newcomer. Each house had just enough room for its occupants, and each branch of the family bore its own troubles. I might well find shelter for a day or a week, but permanent residence would constitute a cancerous growth in any house.

So I would hurry off to the café, my paradisiacal refuge. I would meet up with colleagues and find solace in exchanging complaints. And strange as it may seem, I was regarded among them as one of the lucky ones, being on my own and the load I carried being consequently light. My terrible solitude was something of value, something to be envied. How lucky you are—no wife, no daughter, no son! None of the problems of the generation gap, or of marrying off daughters, or of paying for private lessons. You are in a position to eat meat once a week, or even twice. A home just for yourself, which knows no arguments or quarrels. I would nod my head with satisfaction, but deep down I would wonder whether they had not forgotten the pains of repression and loneliness. Even so I would find in their continual moaning and groaning a certain comfort, like a flash of light being cast upon a tomb.

Once one of them said to me, "I have a solution to all your difficulties." I looked at him intently and waited. "A wedding," [illegible] that will provide you with a home and an easy life, [illegible] worth a penny." Then in a whisper, "A woman befitting your position."

Sometimes I imagined a woman with nothing female about her except being so described on the civil register certificate: an abnormal way of salvation (like perversion and clandestine affairs), a life belt in the shape of a floating corpse. In truth I had lost hope, though I still retained my pride. For this reason they used to describe me as having a good nature, which was a synonym for stupidity.

I would persevere and struggle on. I would return to *The Lives of the Saints*, and read the opposition newspapers. Sometimes, maybe, I would resort to the wiles of spongers—a pardonable offense. I would visit the homes of relatives, but avoiding mealtimes—thus assiduously demonstrating my innocence—yet still in the hope I might be invited to a banquet of a feast. But the spirit of the time no longer believed in such age-old traditions, and what is more, things are now different in relation to feasts and holidays. I am thus lucky if I get one or two good meals a year. On these occasions I would hear the voice of the lady of the house saying, "Don't stand on ceremony. You're not a stranger or a guest. Treat the house as your own." And no sooner would the green light be given than I would swoop down like a ravenous eagle, as though seeing my last meal.

Worse than all this, I was an ordinary person, a person without ambitions or imagination. I had had just sufficient education for the powers-that-be to put me into a certain department. Beyond that all I had hoped for was a nice girl and a small flat. But things did not turn out like that; I don't know why. Thus my place of residence was destined to be the tumbledown house, and whenever my salary was raised I somehow found myself having less money [illegible] It was like one of those [illegible] pose to radio audiences in the [illegible] melted away in inflation, and every day I [illegible] ing waves that threatened to drown me.

Someone said, "Go abroad, there are [illegible] vantages to traveling." But I [illegible] my homeland. However, I did not surrender to [illegible] spair. From time to time in my darkened sky [illegible] gleam of light. I was stimulated by the [illegible] shots fired by the opposition, and anecdotes about [illegible] such as the story that the great jurisprudent [illegible] convulsed with hunger, nevertheless was generous in [illegible] of alms. Sometimes I would amuse myself at my window watching Sitt Fawziyya strutting up and down the ditch [illegible] two sides that were growing ever closer together.

Then one day, after a long absence, I decided to visit the family burial vault, seeing that it was the final place of refuge if things came to the worst. There was, after all, the mourning room, and there was also a lavatory. It was a shelter for someone who had none.

I saw the two old tombs open to the sky and the prickly pears growing in the corners. The mourning room, to the right as one entered, had become a veritable beehive [illegible] with women and children and was piled high with tattered [illegible] kerosene stoves, and pots and pans, the whole place [illegible] garlic sauce, beans, eggplant, and frying [illegible]. The [illegible] garded me with apprehension, and I read [illegible] eyes a warning of challenge. I smiled [illegible] and [illegible] directly in front of them, divested of all power and glory [illegible] addressed a woman whose bulk reminded me of Sitt Fawziyya: "It's all right, but what's to be done if I need the room [illegible] place to live?"

"You're the person with the rights," she answered, laughing, "and we're your guests. We'd give up a corner to you, because after all, people must help one another."

Outwardly showing gratitude, I said, "God bless you."

I went through to the two tombs to recite the opening chapter of the Koran over them. I imagined the many generations of whom nothing remained but skeletons—squadrons of craftsmen and traders and civil servants and housewives. I remembered too an uncle on my mother's side, of whom, although I am not sure exactly when he was born, I have heard recounted the legend of his heroic death in the 1919 Revolution.

I stood for a while in intimate conversation with them in an inaudible voice. "May God have mercy upon you, impart to me your faith. And, Uncle, please give me something of your courage!"

Half a Day

I proceeded alongside my father, clutching his right hand, running to keep up with the long strides he was taking. All my clothes were new: the black shoes, the green school uniform, and the red tarboosh. My delight in my new clothes, however, was not altogether unmarred, for this was no feast day but the day on which I was to be cast into school for the first time.

My mother stood at the window watching our progress, and I would turn toward her from time to time, as though appealing for help. We walked along a street lined with gardens; on both sides were extensive fields planted with crops, prickly pears, henna trees, and a few date palms.

"Why school?" I challenged my father openly. "I shall never do anything to annoy you."

"I'm not punishing you," he said, laughing. "School's not a punishment. It's the factory that makes useful men out of boys. Don't you want to be like your father and brothers?"

I was not convinced. I did not believe there was really any good to be had in tearing me away from the intimacy of my home and throwing me into this building that stood at the end of the road like some huge, high-walled fortress, exceedingly stern and grim.

When we arrived at the gate we could see the courtyard, vast and crammed full of boys and girls. "Go in by yourself," said my father, "and join them. Put a smile on your face and be a good example to others."

I hesitated and clung to his hand, but he gently pushed me

from him. "Be a man," he said. "Today you truly begin life. You will find me waiting for you when it's time to leave."

I took a few steps, then stopped and looked but saw nothing. Then the faces of boys and girls came into view. I did not know a single one of them, and none of them knew me. I felt I was a stranger who had lost his way. But glances of curiosity were directed toward me, and one boy approached and asked, "Who brought you?"

"My father," I whispered.

"My father's dead," he said quite simply.

I did not know what to say. The gate was closed, letting out a pitiable screech. Some of the children burst into tears. The bell rang. A lady came along, followed by a group of men. The men began sorting us into ranks. We were formed into an intricate pattern in the great courtyard surrounded on three sides by high buildings of several floors; from each floor we were overlooked by a long balcony roofed in wood.

"This is your new home," said the woman. "Here too there are mothers and fathers. Here there is everything that is enjoyable and beneficial to knowledge and religion. Dry your tears and face life joyfully."

We submitted to the facts, and this submission brought a sort of contentment. Living beings were drawn to other living beings, and from the first moments my heart made friends with [illegible] my misgivings [illegible] school would have this rich variety. We [illegible] games: swings, the vaulting horse, [illegible] we chanted our first songs. We also had our first introduction to language. We [illegible] numbers.

were told of His present world and of His Hereafter, and we heard examples of what He said. We ate delicious food, took a little nap, and woke up to go on with friendship and love, play and learning.

As our path revealed itself to us, however, we did not find it as totally sweet and unclouded as we had presumed. Dust-laden winds and unexpected accidents came about suddenly, so we had to be watchful, at the ready, and very patient. It was not all a matter of playing and fooling around. Rivalries could bring about pain and hatred or give rise to fighting. And while the lady would sometimes smile, she would often scowl and scold. Even more frequently she would resort to physical punishment.

In addition, the time for changing one's mind was over and gone and there was no question of ever returning to the paradise of home. Nothing lay ahead of us but exertion, struggle, and perseverance. Those who were able took advantage of the opportunities for success and happiness that presented themselves amid the worries.

The bell rang announcing the passing of the day and the end of work. The throngs of children rushed toward the gate, which was opened again. I bade farewell to friends and sweethearts and passed through the gate. I peered around but found no trace of my father, who had promised to be there. I stepped aside to wait. When I had waited for a long time without avail, I decided to return home on my own. After I had taken a few steps, a middle-aged man passed by, and I realized at once that I knew him. He came toward me, smiling, and shook me by the hand, saying, "It's a long time since we last met—how are you?"

With a nod of my head, I agreed with him and in turn asked, "And you, how are you?"

"As you can see, not all that good, the Almighty be praised!"

Again he shook me by the hand and went off. I went a few steps forward, then came to a startled halt.

the street lined with gardens? Where had it disappeared to? When did all these vehicles invade it? And when did all these hordes of humanity come to rest upon its surface? How did these hills of refuse come to cover its sides? And where were the fields that bordered it? High buildings had taken over, the street surged with children, and disturbing noises shook the air. At various points stood conjurers showing off their tricks and making snakes appear from baskets. Then there was a band announcing the opening of a circus, with clowns and weight lifters walking in front. A line of trucks carrying central security troops crawled majestically by. The siren of a fire engine shrieked, and it was not clear how the vehicle would cleave its way to reach the blazing fire. A battle raged between a taxi driver and his passenger, while the passenger's wife called out for help and no one answered. Good God! I was in a daze. My head spun. I almost went crazy. How could all this have happened in half a day, between early morning and sunset? I would find the answer at home with my father. But where was my home? I could see only tall buildings and hordes of people. I hastened on to the crossroads between the gardens and Abu Khoda. I had to cross Abu Khoda to reach my house, but the stream of cars would not let up. The fire engine's siren was shrieking at full pitch as it moved at a snail's pace, and I said to myself, "Let the fire take its pleasure in what it consumes." Extremely irritated, I wondered when I would be able to cross. I stood there a long time, until the young lad employed at the ironing shop on the corner came up to me. He stretched out his arm and said gallantly, "Grandpa, let me take you across."

The Tavern of the Black Cat

They were engaged in a sing-song when a stranger appeared at the door.

There was not a single free chair in the tavern, which consisted of a square room in the basement of an old, dilapidated building. The room looked onto a rear alley through the iron bars of a single window, and its gloomy, tomblike atmosphere required it to be lit both day and night. Its walls had been painted a light blue and they exuded dark stains of dampness in various places. Its door opened onto a long narrow passageway that led to the street, and on one of the room's sides were ranged barrels of the infernal wine. The tavern's patrons were one big family tree whose branches were spread among the bare wooden tables. Some of them were bound by ties of friendship or by being colleagues at work, while all were joined in the brotherhood of being together in the same place and in the spiritual intimacy they shared there night after night. They were united too by conversation and the infernal wine.

They were engaged in a sing-song when a stranger appeared at the door.

It was not uncommon for one of them to be asked the question, "Why is it that you prefer the Tavern of the Black Cat?"

Its real name is The Star, but it acquired its popular name because of its huge black cat, adored by the emaciated and angular Greek owner, and friend and mascot of the patrons.

"I prefer the Tavern of the Black Cat because of its friendly, family atmosphere and because for a piaster or two you can fly without wings."

The black cat would roam about from table to table in search of bread crumbs and scraps of felafel and fish. It would hang about at people's feet and rub itself against their legs with the coquetry of one deprived of God's favors, while its Greek owner would lean his elbows on the table, gazing lifelessly into space. As for the old waiter, he would go around with the wine or fill up the small ribbed glasses from the taps on the barrels.

"And it's the tavern with the most compassion for those with [illegible]ed incomes."

Witticisms and anecdotes would be exchanged, and hearts would grow closer by sharing grievances. Then someone with [illegible] voice would break into song, and that damp, tomblike [illegible] would overflow with happiness.

"There's no harm in our forgetting for a moment the plurality of children and the paucity of money."

"And to forget the heat and the flies . . ."

"And to forget that there's a world outside the iron bars."

"And to take pleasure in fondling the black cat."

In the moments of being together, their spirits would become [illegible] resounding with love for everything, freed from fear and [illegible] and cleansed of the specters of disease, old age, and [illegible]. They would conceive themselves in a likeness to which [illegible]ed, outstripping time by whole centuries.

They were engaged in a sing-song when a stranger appeared [illegible] door.

The stranger looked all around but did not find an empty [illegible]. He disappeared from sight into the passageway, and they [illegible] he had gone for good, but he returned carrying a rush [illegible] the chair of the Greek owner himself—placed it against [illegible] narrow door and sat down.

He had come in with a sullen expression, and had returned [illegible] with one. He looked at no one. His eyes revealed [illegible] a look that was absent, that was taking refuge in some unknown, faraway world and seeing none of those who were filling the small place. His appearance in general was dark, strong, and frightening, as if he were a wrestler, a pugilist, or a weight lifter. And his clothes went perfectly with his dark complexion; they accented it—the black sweater, the dark gray trousers, and the brown rubber-soled shoes. The only thing that shone in that gloomy form was a square-shaped patch of baldness that crowned a large hard-looking head.

His unexpected presence let loose an electric charge that penetrated through to the depths of those seated around the tables. The singing stopped, the expressions on the men's faces contracted, the laughter subsided. Eyes alternated between staring at him and stealing glances at him. This, though, did not last long. Waking from the shock of surprise and terror at his appearance, they refused to allow the stranger to spoil their evening. With gestures they called upon one another to shun him, to continue having a good time. Once again they went back to their conversation, to their joking and drinking, but he was not in fact absent from their consciousness: they did not succeed in ignoring him completely, and he continued to weigh upon their spirits like some inflamed tooth. The man clapped his hands with disquieting loudness, and the aged waiter came and brought him a glass of the infernal wine. He quickly downed it and followed it with a second, then ordered four glasses at once and drained them one after another. Then he ordered more. A sensation of fear and awe came over them, the laughter died on their lips; they withdrew into a dejected silence. What sort of man was this? The amount of wine he had consumed was enough to have killed an elephant, and here he was sitting like a solid rock, wholly unaffected, his features unrelaxed. What sort of man was this?

The black cat approached tentatively. It waited for some [illegible] cat began rubbing itself against his leg. But the man stamped on the ground and the cat retreated, no doubt amazed at such treatment, the like of which it had never before experienced. The Greek turned his lifeless face toward the sound. He regarded the stranger at length, then went back to looking at nothing. The stranger emerged from his state of inertia. He moved his head to right and left violently, bit on his lips, then began talking in an inaudible voice, either to himself or to some person of his imagination. He menaced and threatened, waving his fist about. His face took on the ugliest expression of anger. The silence and fear were intense.

His voice was heard for the first time, a harsh voice like the bellowing of a beast.

"Curses . . . doom and destruction . . ." he repeated loudly.

He clenched his fist and continued. "Let the mountain come down—and what's behind the mountain."

He was silent for a while, then went on talking in a voice slightly less loud, "This is the question, quite simply and frankly."

They became convinced that there was no point staying on any longer. When it had hardly begun, he had ruined the evening's entertainment. They might as well go off peacefully. Agreement was reached among them with an exchange of looks, then there was a general movement of getting ready and standing up. It was then that, for the first time, he took notice of them. Emerging from his trance, he let his gaze move among them questioningly. With a gesture he halted them as he asked, "Who are you?"

The question deserved to be ignored and treated with contempt. But no one thought to ignore it or treat it with contempt.

"For a long time we've been patrons of the place," answered one of them, taking heart from his mature years.

"When did you come?"

"We came at the beginning of the evening."

"Then you were here before I arrived?"

"Yes."

He gestured to them to return to their places.

"No one is to leave the room," he said sternly.

They could not believe their ears. They were tongue-tied with amazement, but not one of them dared to answer him as he deserved. The middle-aged man, with a calmness not at all consistent with his feelings, said, "But we want to go."

He threw them a stony, threatening glare. "Let him who has no care for his life advance!"

There was no one among them who had no care for his life. They exchanged dazed, baffled glances.

"But what's the purpose of your objecting to our leaving?" asked the middle-aged man.

The stranger shook his head with grim scorn. "Don't try to fool me," he said. "You have heard everything. . . ."

"I can assure you we have heard nothing," said the middle-aged man in astonishment.

"Don't try to fool me," he shouted angrily. "You've learned what it's all about."

"We heard nothing and we know nothing."

"Deceiving liars!"

"You must believe us."

"Believe riotous drunkards?"

"You are insulting innocent people and sullying their honor."

"Let him who has no care for his life advance!"

It became plain to them that the situation could only be handled by force, and this was something they could not muster. Under the spell of his fearsome gaze, they were obliged to return to their seats with suppressed anger and an unprecedented sense of degradation.

"And how long shall we remain here?" asked the old man.

"Until the appropriate time comes."

"And when will the appropriate time come?"

"Shut up and wait."

The time passed in painful tension. As they sat subdued by distress and worry, the wine flew from their heads. Even the black cat was conscious of a hostile odor in the atmosphere, so it jumped up onto the ledge of the sole window, then lay down, folded its front paws beneath its head, and closed its eyes, allowing its tail to hang out between the bars.

Certain questions about the man demanded to be answered. Was he drunk? Was he mad? What was the story he was accusing them of having heard? During all this time the Greek owner persisted in his lifeless silence, while the waiter, as though he were seeing and hearing nothing, went on serving the stranger.

The stranger began to look at them with scornful malice, then he said menacingly, "If any one of you has the idea of playing me false, I'll punish the lot of you mercilessly."

They took heart when he resumed talking, so the middle-aged man said with evident sincerity, "I swear to you, we all swear to you . . ."

"If I asked you for an oath, by what would you swear?"

A tiny hope invaded them, and the middle-aged man said eagerly, "By what you want—by our children, by the Almighty!"

"Nothing has any value with patrons of such a vulgar tavern!"

"We're not as you think, we're decent fathers and faithful believers. That may be just why we so need to refresh our burdened spirits. . . ."

"Depraved scoundrels, you are dreaming of building castles not by hard work but by the contemptible exploitation of the story!"

"We swear by God Almighty that we do not know of the story and have no idea what it's about."

"Who of you is without a story, you cowards?"

"You did not speak. Your lips were moving, but no sound came from them," said the old man.

"Do not try to deceive me, you old dodderer!"

"You must believe us and let us be."

"Woe to you if you make a move! Woe to you if you act treacherously! If it comes to it, I'll smash your heads and I'll use them to block up the passageway."

The man was truly fearsome, maybe also fearful, which would in itself increase the possibility of things ending badly. Despair crept into their hearts like a wave of deadly cold. He did not stop drinking, though he did not get drunk or become listless or torpid. And here he was, barring the sole way out of the place, powerful, violent, and as steely as the bars at the window.

They went on hopelessly exchanging glances. Whenever they glimpsed a shadow behind the bars, hope sprang to their hearts, though they were unable to make the slightest movement. Even the black cat seemed to have deserted them completely, and continued to enjoy its slumbers. One of them, finding the restraint too hard to bear, asked apprehensively, "Can I go to the toilet?"

"Who told you I was a wet nurse!"

The old man sighed and said, "Are we fated to remain like this till morning?"

"You'll be lucky to see the morning!"

To argue was futile: the man was mad or on the run or both. There might be some story behind him or there might be nothing at all. Despite their number they were prisoners. He was strong and powerful, and they possessed neither strength nor determination. Was there, though, no way of resisting? No possibility of resistance of any kind?

Once again they exchanged glances. Concern was to be seen in their eyes, and whisperings, just discreet enough for the stranger not to hear, were passed between them.

"What a disaster!"

"What a humiliation!"

"What ignominy!"

And suddenly a glance was embellished with something that resembled a smile, was in fact an actual smile. Was it really a smile?

"Why not? It's a funny situation."

"Funny?"

"Look at it with passing objectivity and you'll find it's enough to make you die laughing!"

"Really?"

"I'm frightened I'll explode with laughter."

"Remember," said the middle-aged man in a voice that was only just audible, "that the time we normally leave is still a long way off."

"But there's no longer any real evening gathering."

"Because we've discontinued it without reason."

"Without reason?"

"I mean without a reason to prevent us continuing as of now."

"And in what sort of humor would we go on with it after what has happened?"

"Let's forget the door for a while and see what's what."

No one welcomed the suggestion and no one rejected it. The glasses of infernal wine were produced. Though this was in front of the stranger's eyes, he paid the men no attention. They drank too much, heads became dizzy, and they were carried away in their intoxication. Magically their worries were lifted and their laughter rang out. They danced on the chairs, capped each other's jokes, and sang "Good news is here of friendship's feast."

And all the time they ignored the door. They completely forgot its existence. The black cat awoke and began moving from table to table, from leg to leg. They drank to excess, they enjoyed themselves to excess, they became boisterous to excess, as though savoring the last of their nights at the tavern.

A miracle occurred, for the present retreated and melted away in a rising flood of forgetfulness; memory dissolved, and everything that it had stored away in its cells was demolished. No one knew his companion. The wine was truly infernal, and yet, yes and yet . . .

"But where are we?"

"Tell me who we are and I'll tell you where we are."

"There was some singing."

"Or was it, as I remember, weeping?"

"There was some story. I wonder what story it was?"

"And this black cat, it is without doubt something tangible."

"Yes, it is the thread that will bring us to the truth."

"Here we are, getting close to the truth."

"This cat was a god at the time of our forefathers."

"And one day it seated itself at the door of a prison cell and made known the secret of the story."

"And it threatened woe."

"But what's the story?"

"Originally there was a god, then it was changed into a cat."

"But what's the story?"

"How can a cat talk?"

"Did it not divulge to us the story?"

"Indeed, but we wasted the time in singing and weeping."

"And so the threads came together and the way was cleared for grasping the truth."

The voice of the old waiter was raised as he scolded someone, threatening and shouting, "Wake up, you idle wretch, or I'll smash your head in."

A huge man, his head bent in dejection, came along. He began taking up the glasses and dishes, cleaning the tables, and collecting the refuse from the floor. Immersed in a deep sadness, with his eyes bathed in tears, he worked without uttering a word or looking at anyone. With mournful compassion they followed him with their eyes. One of them asked him, "What's the story?"

But he did not turn, and continued with his work, silent and sad, his eyes streaming with tears.

"When and where have I seen this man?" the middle-aged man asked himself.

The man, with his dark clothes composed of a black sweater, dark gray trousers, and brown rubber-soled shoes, made his way toward the passageway. Again the middle-aged man asked himself, "When and where have I seen this man?"

The Lawsuit

I found myself suddenly the subject of a lawsuit. My father's widow was demanding maintenance. Awakened from the depths of time, the past with its memories had invaded me. After reading the petition I exclaimed, "When did she go broke? Has she in her turn been robbed?"

"This woman robbed us and deprived us of our legal rights," I said to my lawyer.

I felt a strong desire to see her, not through any temptation to gloat over her but in order to see what effects time had had upon her. Today, like me, she was in her forties. Had her beauty withstood the passage of time? Was it holding out against poverty? If the lawsuit was not genuine, would she have stretched out a demanding hand to one of her enemies? On the other hand, if it was specious, why had she not stretched out her hand before? What a ravishing beauty she had been!

"My father married her," I told the lawyer, "when he was in his middle fifties and she a girl of twenty." A semiliterate, old-fashioned contractor, he did not deal with banks but stored his profits away in a large cupboard in his bedroom. We were happy about this so long as we were a single family. The announcement of the new marriage was like a bomb exploding among us—my mother, my elder brother, and myself, as well as my sisters in their various homes. The top floor was given over to my father, the bride, and the cupboard. We were struck dumb by her youth and beauty. My mother said in a quavering voice choked with weeping, "What a catastrophe! We'll end up without a bean."

My elder brother was illiterate and mentally retarded. He was without work, but considered himself a landowner. He flared up in a rage, declaring, "I'll defend myself to the very death."

Some of our relatives advised us to consult a lawyer, but my father threatened my mother with divorce if we were to entertain any such move. "I'm not gullible or an idiot, and no one's rights will be lost."

I was the one least affected by the disaster, partly because of my youth and partly because I was the only one in the family who wanted to study, hoping to enter the engineering college. Yet even so, I did not miss the significance of the facts—my father's age and that of his beautiful bride, and the fortune under threat. By way of smoothing things over, I would say, "I have confidence in my father."

"If we say nothing," my brother would say, "we'll find the cupboard empty."

I shared his fears but affected outwardly what I did not feel inwardly. All the time I felt that our oasis, which had appeared so tranquil, was being subjected to a wild wind and that on the horizon black clouds were gathering. My mother took refuge in silent anxiety, with each new day giving her warning of a bad outcome. As for my elder brother, he would brave the lion in his lair, pleading with his father. "I am the firstborn, uneducated as you can see, and without means of support, so give me my share."

"Do you want to inherit from me while I'm still alive? It's a disgrace for you to doubt me—no one's rights will be lost." But my brother would not calm down and would pester my father whenever they met. He would hurl threats at him from behind his back, and my mother would say that she was more worried about my brother than she was about the fortune.

For my part, I wondered whether my father, that capable

master of his trade, the man who was such a meticulous accountant despite his illiteracy, would meet defeat at the hands of a pretty girl. Yet, without doubt, he was changing, slipping down little by little each day. He would take himself off to the Turkish baths twice a month, would clip his beard and trim his mustache every week, and would strut about in new clothes. Finally he took to dyeing his hair. Precious gifts embellished the bride's neck, bosom, and arms. Now there was a Chevrolet and a chauffeur waiting in front of our house.

My brother became more and more angry. "Where did he get her from?" he would say to me. Was it so impossible that she might get hold of the key and find her way to opening the cupboard? Would she not take from him something to secure her future? Did she not have the power to make him happy or to turn his life into one of misery and turmoil as she wished?

Arguments would develop between my brother and my father that would go beyond the bounds of propriety. My father would grow angry and spit in my brother's face. In an explosive outburst, my brother seized hold of a table lamp and hurled it at his father, drawing blood. Seeing the blood, my brother was scared, but even so persevered in his attempts to do Father in, with the cook and the chauffeur intervening. My father insisted on informing the police, and my brother was taken off to court and from there to prison, where he died after a year.

"How did she find the courage to bring her case?" I asked the lawyer.

"Necessity has its own rules."

In the midst of our alarm and our mourning for my brother, my mother and I heard the noise of something striking the floor above us. We hurried upstairs and found ourselves standing aghast over my father's body. As is usual in such circumstances, we asked ourselves again and again what could have happened, but no amount of questioning can bring back the dead. It seems that he had had a paralyzing stroke a whole day before his death without our knowing.

We waited till he had been buried and the rites of mourning were over, and then the family gathered together. My sisters, their husbands, and their husbands' parents were there, and the lawyer was present as well. We asked about the key to the cupboard, and the young widow answered quite simply that she knew nothing about it. Sometimes the mind boggles at the sheer brazenness of lying. But what could be done? We then came across the key, and the cupboard finally divulged its secrets, exhibiting to us with profound mockery a bundle of notes that did not exceed five thousand pounds. "Then where is the man's fortune?" everyone called out.

All eyes were fixed on the beautiful widow, who answered defiantly. We had recourse to the police, and there were investigations and searches. As my mother had predicted, we came out of it all "without a bean." The beautiful widow went off to her parents' house, and the curtain was brought down upon her and the inheritance. My mother died. I got a job, married, and achieved a notable success. I became oblivious of the past until the lawsuit brought me back to it.

"It's really the height of irony," I said to the lawyer, "that I should be required to pay maintenance to that woman."

His voice came to me from between the files on his desk. "The old story does on the face of it appear worthy of being put forward, but what's the point of unearthing it when we have no evidence against her?"

"Even if the old story may not be open for discussion, it's a good starting point, whose effect should not be underrated."

"On the contrary, we would be providing the woman's lawyer with the chance to take the offensive and to attract sympathy for her."

"Sympathy?"

"Steady now. Let's think about it a bit objectively. An old man hoards his wealth in a cupboard in his bedroom. He then buys himself a beautiful girl of twenty when he's a man of fifty-five. Such and such happens to his family and such and such to his beautiful wife. Fine, who was to blame?" He was silent for a while, scowling, then continued. "Let's look at it from your side. You're a man who's earning and has a family, and the cost of living is unbearably high, and so on and so forth. . . . Let's content ourselves by settling on a reasonable sum for maintenance."

"Too bad!" I muttered. "She robbed us; then there was the death of my brother and my mother's distress."

"I'm sorry about that, but she's as much a victim as you are. Even the fortune she made off with brought her to disaster. And now here she is begging."

Prompted by casual curiosity, I said, "It's as though you know something about her."

He shook his head with diplomatic vagueness. "A woman who couldn't have children, she was married and divorced several times when she was in her prime. In middle age she fell in love with a student, who, in his turn, robbed her and went off."

He did not divulge the sources of his information, but I surmised the logical progression of events. I experienced a feeling of gratification, which a sense of decency prevented me from showing.

On the day of the court session, I was again seized by a mysterious desire to set eyes on her. I recognized her as she waited in front of the lawyers' room. I knew her by conjecture before actually recognizing her, for the beauty that had made away with our fortune and ruined us had completely vanished. She was fat, excessively and unacceptably so, and the charming freshness had leaked away from her face. What little beauty was left seemed insipid. A veneer of perpetual dejection acted like a screen between her and other people. Without giving the matter any thought, I went up to her, inclined my head in greeting, and said, "I remember you . . . perhaps you remember me?"

At first she gazed at me in surprise, then in confusion. She returned the greeting with a gesture of her covered head. "I'm sorry to cause you trouble," she said, as though apologizing, "but I am forced to do so."

I forgot what I wanted to say. In fact words failed me, and I felt an inner peace. "Don't worry—let the Lord do as He wills." I quietly moved away as I said to myself, "Why not? Even a farce must continue right to the final act."

The Empty Café

Mohammed Rasheedi, in a tone shaky with sorrow and emotion, said, "To the mercy of God the Merciful, to the proximity of your noble Lord, O Zahia, my life's companion. To the mercy of God I commend you."

He sobbed as he bent over the body laid out on the bed, leaning, through his great weariness, with his right hand on the pillow, until the old servant woman took pity on him, gently patted his hand, and took him from her who lay dead into the sitting room, where he sank with loud sighs into an armchair. He stretched out his legs, moaning, then mumbled, "Now I'm alone, without a companion. Why did you leave me, Zahia? After being together for forty years, why did you go before me, Zahia?"

The servant consoled him with trite phrases, though the sight of the old man in his nineties weeping was a truly sad one. His furrowed cheeks and pitted nose gleamed with tears. The servant left the room, struggling with her own tears. He closed his eyes, on the rims of which there was only the occasional single eyelash. "Forty years ago I married you," he continued, "when you were still in your twenties. I educated you myself, and we were very happy despite the difference in age. You were the best of companions, you kindly person—so I commend you to the mercy of God."

For his age, he was in excellent health, tall and thin. The surface of his face had completely disappeared under wrinkles and furrows, while the bones protruded sharply, skull-like.

Deep within his eyes there lurked a gaze beneath a pale veil on which the visible things of this world were not reflected.

The funeral was attended by many people, not one of whom was a friend or acquaintance of his. They came to give their condolences to his son, or in deference to his daughter's husband, employed at an embassy abroad. As for him, not a single friend of his was still alive. He went on welcoming the faces that were unknown to him and asking himself where the first generation of educators were. Where were the real politicians from the time of Mustafa Kamil and Mohammed Farid?

When the obsequies were concluded around midnight, his son Sabir asked him, "What do you intend doing, Father?"

His son's wife said, "It's not possible for you to stay on here alone."

The old man understood what they meant. He complained, "Zahia was everything to me. She was my mind and my hand."

"My house is yours," said Sabir, "and if you came to live with us you would bring a blessing to it. Your servant Mubarka will come to look after you."

Certainly he could not live in this house on his own. Yet despite the kindness shown by his son and his son's wife, he believed that by moving he would be losing a lot of his freedom and authority. But what was to be done? In his youth and early manhood, he had been a robust person, and he still retained his dignified bearing. How many generations of educators and outstanding personalities had he trained—but what was to be done?

With a dejected air, the man witnessed the liquidation of his home. He saw it being demolished, just as he had seen the death of his wife, and they left nothing intact but his clothes, his bed, his cupboard of books (books he no longer looked at), some bibelots, and pictures of members of the family and of certain great men of literature, politics, and entertainment, like Mustafa

Kamil, Mohammed Farid, al-Muwailhi, Hafiz Ibrahim, and Abd al-Hayy Helmi.

He left his house for Heliopolis in his son's car. A bedroom had been prepared for him, and the old servant Mubarka got ready to serve him. "We're all at your beck and call," his son said.

Munira, Sabir's wife, gave him a welcoming smile. It showed a kindly disposition, but this was still not his house—that was his overwhelming feeling. He sat in an armchair, exchanging glances with her in an almost embarrassed way. If only his daughter Samira were in Egypt. He would have found a more congenial atmosphere in her house. Tutu appeared in the doorway. He looked from one of his parents to the other, then ran and clung to his father's legs. He regarded his grandfather, and the old man smiled and said, "Hullo, Tutu. Come here."

It was only occasionally that Tutu would go with his father to visit his grandfather. The old man loved him very much and did not spare himself in playing with the boy whenever possible, though Tutu was violent in his fun. He used to like to jump on those who were playing with him, and would threaten to scratch their eyes and nose. All too soon the old man would gently avoid him, preferring to love him from afar.

Tutu pointed at his grandfather's tall tarboosh. "Your head!"

He meant that the old man should take off his tarboosh so that Tutu could see the sloping oblong of orange baldness that had drawn his attention and inquiries from the first time he had seen it. When his wish was not fulfilled, he began pointing at his grandfather's furrowed face and pitted nose, and went on asking questions despite his father's attempts to shut him up. The old man told himself that the dear child would not cease to annoy him and that he required protection. But where was Zahia? And his watch, his flyswatter, and his cigarettes—how would he keep them out of the reach of the boy's prying hands?

Tutu tried to get to his grandfather to implement his wishes himself, but his father caught hold of him and called the nurse, who carried him off, screaming in protest.

"When I finish work in the evenings," said Sabir, "Munira and I go to the club, so why don't you come with us?"

"Don't bother yourself about me. Just let things go on as usual."

Sabir and Munira went off, and the old man welcomed being left on his own so that he could recover. But being alone became more quickly tedious than he had imagined. He cast an indifferent glance at the room and was then enwrapped by loneliness. When would he become accustomed to the new place and to life without Zahia? For forty years he had not seen a day go by without Zahia. Since she was brought to him in marriage in Helmiyya, and Sarrafiyya had danced before them, the house under her direction had enjoyed an ordered cleanliness, with its fragrant smell of incense. What was the point of Ramadan and the feasts without her?

The funeral had been lacking generation upon generation of his students. Did nobody remember him anymore?

This had not been so with the friends who had departed long ago. But though they were gone, it seemed he saw every one of them as on the day they had been brought together at Mustafa Kamil's funeral.

While the old man had never known any serious illness, his poor wife had been afflicted by dengue fever, typhoid, and bouts of influenza, and she had finally died from a heart condition, leaving him as attached to life as he had always been. He went to a window and saw a large garden in the middle of a rectangle of buildings, instead of the large mosque he used to be able to see from the window of his room in Munira's house. A warm dry breeze blew against him. He enjoyed the restful silence, though it accentuated his loneliness. The day the British had occupied Cairo, he had got hold of a stray horse, but his father, fearing the consequences, had beaten him and had taken the horse by night to the Cairo Canal, where he had let it loose. The city had been shaking with fear and sorrow.

Returning to where he had been sitting, he saw a small cat by the foot of the chair. It was pure white, with a thick coat and a black patch on its forehead. In the look in its gray eyes he saw a willingness to make friends. Zahia had always had a fondness for cats. Liking the look of it, he followed it with his eyes as it moved around the chair leg. He stroked its back, and it rubbed itself against his foot, making him smile. He passed his hand along its back, and it answered the palm of his hand. Its back throbbed, rising and falling. He took this as a sign of affection and once again smiled, revealing teeth with moss-colored roots, while the cat arched with pleasure. He shifted to his left slightly to give it room, but Tutu's voice, tremulous with the effort of running, blared out as he rushed into the room. "My cat!"

Resigned, the old man said, "Here's your cat," and asked him affectionately about its name.

"Nargis," answered the boy gruffly, as he seized hold of it roughly by the scruff of the neck and ran off outside with it, while the old man pleaded, "Gently . . . gently. . . ."

Suddenly he jumped. What in heaven's name had happened? It seemed that something had struck him on the forehead. He frowned with annoyance, and Tutu's laughter rang out from the doorway as he picked up the small ball that had bounced back to him. The old man put his hand up to feel his glasses and make sure they were all right, then he called Mubarka, who hurried along and carried off the child before he could throw the ball again.

"This dear child is tiresome and cruel. That poor unfortunate cat!"

Five years ago his daughter Samira had lost a child of Tutu's age, and he had consoled her with tears. "It is I who should have died. . . ." It had seemed to him, as he sat at the funeral, that all eyes were contemplating his old age in amazement, pointing out the glaring contradiction between his own survival and the passing away of his grandson at the age of three. That night he had said to Zahia, "A long life is a curse." But how gentle she was as she said to him, "We'd all do anything for you—you're a bringer of good luck and fortune."

Late in the afternoon, on his return from work, Sabir said to his father, "Seeing that you don't want to go with us to the club, choose yourself some café in Heliopolis. We have fine cafés quite near the house."

While choosing a café nearby was perhaps the sensible thing to do, he liked the Mattatia. It had been his favorite place for a very long time. He made his way to the bus stop, walking at his own slow pace but with his body held erect. He used a stick but did not support his weight on it. Many people looked at him in astonishment, an astonishment mingled with admiration.

He took his place in the café under the arcades, as he said to himself half-jokingly, "Why's the café so empty?" The café was not in fact empty, and very few tables were unoccupied. It was, though, empty of any friends or acquaintances. It was his habit to gaze at the chairs that had been used by dear departed friends of old, and to bring to mind their faces and movements, and the discussions: of the news carried in *al-Muqattam;* of the hotly contested games of backgammon; and of politics. God had decreed that he should walk in their funeral processions, one after the other, and should mourn them all. The time came when one sole companion remained, Ali Pasha Mahran.

This was the chair where he used to sit. Short, thin, and hunched over his stick, with the brim of his tarboosh touching his bushy white eyebrows, staring out at his friend with a fragile, half-tearful look from behind dark blue-tinted glasses, he would ask, "I wonder which of us will outlive the other?" Then he would guffaw with laughter. At that time his hands had the permanent shaking of old age although he was two years the old man's junior.

When Ali Pasha Mahran had died at the age of eighty-five, the old man had grieved a long time. Afterward the world had become empty, the café too.

Here was Ataba Square, gyrating as usual before his dulled eyes, but it was a new square. As for Mattatia, there was not a sign of its original self but the site. Where too was its friendly Greek owner? And the waiter with the handlebar mustache? And the solidly built chairs, the sparkling white marble tables, the polished mirrors, and the buffet with its soft drinks and narghiles—where were all these?

On the night of the Shamm al-Nesim holiday in 1930, the old man had retired. He had spent the evening at the Ezbekiyya Theater with a group of friends, in an atmosphere of merriment and music. And he had spent the following day at the Barrages, celebrating the end of work, and Sheikh Ibrahim Zanati, the Arabic language inspector, had delivered a poem composed for the occasion. That night the old man had had so much brandy he had become drunk as he sat listening enraptured to the voice singing, "O friendship of the beautiful past." When at the end of the night he had gone to sleep, he had dreamed that he was playing in Paradise. Ibrahim Zanati had expressed the wish in his poem that his colleague might enjoy a long life of a hundred years. It seemed that the wish was going to be granted, though the café was empty now, and Sheikh Zanati had passed on while still in his post. The waiter came to take away the tray, but retreated apologetically, reminding the old man of the forgotten and untouched cup of coffee.

When he returned to the house he found it quietly sleeping, its owner not yet back from the club. He found his supper of yogurt on the dining room table. Without assistance he changed out of his clothes with slow laboriousness. Then, sitting down to his supper, he remembered Nargis. If only the kitten would share his supper with him! How lovely it would be to make friends with it and have it for a real companion in this house so preoccupied with itself! Perhaps it was somewhere in the house. He leaned slightly toward the door and called, "Puss . . . Puss." Then he went out and called, "Nargis . . . Puss . . . Puss." A meowing came from behind the door of the room next to his own, where Tutu and his nurse slept. After some thought he approached the door and gently opened it, and the cat passed through, its plump tail held erect like a flag.

Pleased, the old man went back to his room with the cat following him, but an angry shout rang out from Tutu. So, he thought, smiling, the little boy had not been soundly asleep. Tutu came running in and pounced on the cat, grabbing it violently by the neck. His grandfather patted him on the head and said pleasantly, "Hold her gently, Tutu."

But the small boy tightened his grip until it seemed to the old man that Nargis would be throttled. "You go, and I'll bring her to you in bed," he pleaded.

But Tutu would not listen, so the old man bent down and released the cat from the child's grip, saying, "I'll feed her, then bring her back to you."

Tutu jumped up angrily and pushed against his grandfather's knees. The old man staggered, then took an uncertain step backward, swayed, and would have fallen had it not been that the wall supported him. With the cat still on his arm, he remained in his tilted position, unable to right himself. His head was reeling slightly. He pressed his foot down onto the floor and his shoulder against the wall in order to straighten himself but was unable to do so. The cat crawled up his arm to rest on his raised shoulder. Despite the slight dizziness in his head, he realized the danger that threatened his bones. With such strength as he had left, he called out, "Mubarka!"

Tutu was screaming and threatening a fresh onslaught. The old man despaired of saving himself. More fatigued than ever, he was incapable of calling out again. Tutu prepared himself to jump up to where the cat had sought refuge, and hurled himself forward with all his strength. But, rushing out of her room, her eyes dazed with sleep, his nanny caught him by the waist. Then at last Mubarka came, awakened by all the uproar, and ran toward her master, calling out to God in her distress.

She grabbed hold of him from behind and gently righted him, while he moaned. He stood motionless as a statue, and Nargis jumped to the floor and fled. With great difficulty the old man, leaning on Mubarka's arm, returned to his armchair. Some time passed as he sat there in silence with the woman ceaselessly asking him how he was. He motioned with his hand to set her mind at rest, then leaned his head against the back of the chair, his legs stretched out, breathing deeply. He closed his eyes to collect himself.

All at once he remembered a commemorative celebration in honor of someone who had died, a memory deeply rooted in his soul. He had returned from the platform after delivering an appropriate speech and had sat down beside a friend. The friend had leaned across and whispered some complimentary words in his ear. But who was that friend? Ah, he was confident he would bring him back to mind. How distressed he was to have forgotten him! The friend had said something that likewise he could not possibly forget. He would certainly recall it. The clapping and cheering rang out. The meowing of cats grew louder, every eye wept. He could hear the shouting of children. Once again his friend leaned over toward him and spoke. He was sure that he would take possession of the memories, of all of them.

And in no time he had sunk into sleep.

A Day for Saying Goodbye

Life was going on with all its clamor, just as though nothing had happened. Every human being embraces his own secret, possesses it on his own. I cannot be the only one. If the inclinations of the inner self were to assume concrete form, crimes and acts of heroism would be rife. For myself, the experience has come to an end, all because of a blind impulse. Nothing remains but a farewell outing.

At the crossroads, emotions flare up, memories are resurrected. How great is my distress! An extraordinary strength is required to control myself, otherwise the moments of saying goodbye will disappear. Look and enjoy everything, move from place to place, for in every corner there is some forgotten happiness that you must bring to mind. What a crushing blow, filled with bitterness, fury, and hate! I have plunged headlong recklessly, quite oblivious of the consequences. A life that was not bad has been scattered to the winds. Look and remember, be happy, then be sad. For reasons there is no time to enumerate, the angel turned into a devil. How often decay afflicts everything that is good! Love had been uprooted from my heart and it had turned to stone. Let us ignore all that in the short time that remains. What a crushing blow! Of what significance was it?

Port Said Street stirs under an umbrella of white autumnal clouds. The fumes that rise from my chest darken the beauty of things. The nostalgic beckonings from the distant past rap at the doors of my heart. My feet drag me to pay a visit to my sister. Her calm pallid face gazes at me from behind the door. It lights up with happiness. "A rare and unexpected pleasure at this early hour," she says.

She went off to make the coffee, and I sat down to wait in the living room. Our parents and brothers and sisters, who had passed away, looked down at me from their photographs hanging above the tables. No one was left to me except this widowed sister who, being childless, had given her abundant love to me and to Samira and Gamal. Had I come here to commit my son and daughter to her care? She returned with the coffee. She wore a white dressing gown. "Why didn't you go to the office?"

"I took the day off because I felt out of sorts."

"You don't look well—is it a cold?"

"Yes."

"Don't neglect yourself."

My face had begun to betray me. What, I wondered, was now happening in my unhappy flat?

"Yesterday Samira and Gamal paid me a visit."

"They love you just as you love them."

"And how is Seham?"

What an innocent question!

"She's fine."

"Haven't things got better between you?"

"I don't think so."

"I'm always nice to her but I feel she's uneasy with me."

I was seized with grief and kept silent.

"The times we live in need patience and wisdom."

I wanted to ask her to look after Samira and Gamal, but how to do so? Later she would realize the import of my visit. Would Samira and Gamal forgive me for what I had done? How great is my distress!

"What if I went with you now to the doctor's?"

"That's not necessary, Siddiqa. I've got to go and do certain jobs."

"How can I be sure you're all right?"

"I'll visit you tomorrow."

Tomorrow? Once again I am walking in the street. Look and enjoy, and move from place to place. The Sporting Club beach is solitary, devoid of human beings, the waves clapping out their summons and no one answering. The heart beats under the tightly closed envelope of worries. The moment she emerged from the water with her slim body, the skin tinged by the sun's gossamer, she wrapped herself in her beach robe and hurried to the cabin to seat herself by her parents' feet. I was walking by, in shorts, and our eyes met. I was pervaded by a sensation of pleasure to which my heart responded. A voice called to me, and I answered and thus found myself in her company, for the person who had called was her uncle, a colleague of mine in the firm. We were introduced, and some casual conversation between us followed—but how enjoyable it was! Moments of sheer unadulterated happiness, moments that were not to be repeated, moments that refused to be repeated. Now they circle around my heart in the form of a passing yearning that has its warm existence despite the fact that the threads that one day bound them to reality have been torn apart. And her saying that day, "You've a good heart and that is something beyond price." Was it true? Who, then, was it who said that there was no one more vile and despicable than you? And who was it who said that the Lord had created you to torture her and make her miserable? Love should have risen up and stood against the disparities of temperament, but it was the disparities that had put an end to love. Each of us had been stubborn, we had each had as our slogan All or nothing. You were crazy about inane outward appearances and would shout at me saying I was retarded. In terror Samira and Gamal would take refuge in their rooms. How greatly we had harmed them! The love between us had suffered hour by hour and day by day till it breathed its last. It had been choked in the hubbub of continuing arguments, quarrels, and exchanges of abuse. Yet it was in this outdoor café, in this actual corner, that I had disclosed to her uncle my admiration for her.

"Though she hasn't been to university, she is well-educated. Her father had his own policy. After completing her secondary education, the girl was prepared by him for being a housewife, in view of her being sufficiently well provided for."

"That's very convenient," I had said.

He had invited us both to dinner at Santa Lucia, and afterward we had met in the Pelican Garden. The days of courtship, of dreams and impeccable behavior. I hear a beautiful, rapturous tune, though all the strings on which it was played have been broken. What a crushing blow! What is happening in the flat now? Why isn't life made up of perpetual days of courtship? Oh, the masks of lies we hide behind! A salutary method of knowing oneself is indispensable.

"Mr. Mustafa Ibrahim?"

I looked at the man who was calling my name and found him to be an inspector at the firm, no doubt on his way to work. "Hullo, Amr Bey."

"On holiday?"

"Slightly unwell."

"It's only too clear. Would you like me to give you a lift somewhere?"

"No thanks."

He was perhaps the first witness. No, my neighbor the doctor had already seen me as I left the flat. Had he noticed anything unusual? The concierge had seen me too. That was of no importance. I had never thought of making my escape. I would be waiting until the end. Had it not been for my final eagerness to say goodbye, I would have gone by myself.

It was not possible to discard life of my own accord. It had been wrenched from me by force. I had never sought this ending. I had still five years to go before I was fifty. Despite the suffering, life was sweet. Seham had not been able to make it hateful to me. Should I visit Samira and Gamal at the College of Science? They had left without my seeing them, and I had not foreseen what had occurred. I would not find the courage to look them in the eye. It pained me to leave them to their fate. I could imagine them knocking at the door and their mother not hastening to open it. The day would leave its mark until the end of life. And if they cursed me, they would be entitled to do so.

When would I put my grief behind me and dedicate myself to saying goodbye? Look and enjoy, and move from place to place. The market. The day we walked in the market to make our purchases. A man with a bride feels that he is about to take possession of the world itself, feels that happiness may be anything in the world—but not like methylated spirit that just evaporates. With love I say, "To San Giovanni." And she says joyfully, "I'll phone Mummy."

Graciousness, sweetness, and angelic gentleness during our first days together. When and how had the new Seham made her appearance? After becoming a mother, but not at any precisely definable time. How had the sensation of dashed hopes taken control of me? Samira once said, "How quickly and violently you become angry, Father." And I once admitted to Seham, "I may forget myself when I get angry, but it's always for a good reason."

"And for no reason. It's a misunderstanding."

"You squander our life on trivialities."

"Trivialities? You don't understand life."

"You're autocratic. You set no store by reason. What you have in your head must come about regardless of anything."

"Had I respected your opinions we would have been in a real mess."

Look and enjoy, and move from place to place. Abu Qir is the ideal summer resort. Let's have a fish lunch. Fill your stomach and stimulate it with some white wine. We sat together at this place, and here we taught Samira and Gamal to swim when they were young. It is said that despair is one of the two states of rest. Would it not have been better to divorce her?

"Divorce me and set me free."

"I'd like nothing better, if it weren't for my concern for Samira and Gamal."

"You should rather have some concern for yourself and realize that you're an unbearable person."

The truth is that I often wished for your death. However, the fates are not in my hand. Any hardships are easy to bear alongside the hellfire of my hatred. We exchange hatred without making a secret of it. After exchanging the most awful and cruel words, how is it that I am able to partake of my food with appetite? Truly, despair possesses a happiness that is not to be underrated. From the radio issued the song "I, the torment, and your love," and my heart trembled. It was a song I came to love greatly during that fraudulent month of honeymoon. How is it that happiness vanishes after being stronger than existence itself? It is dispersed from the heart and attaches itself to the atmosphere of places after its starting point has been erased. Then, like a bird, it alights on dry ground, adorning it with the embroidery of its wings for several seconds. *I, the torment, and your love*—and this crushing blow.

Perhaps it was the day that, in your madness, you hurled yourself at Samira. In fear I pushed you from her, and you fell and hit your head. There gleamed in your eyes an inhuman look that spat out poison. "I hate you."

"So what?"

"I hate you until death."

"Go to hell."

"Once my heart is disturbed how impossible for it to become cloudless!"

It is, unfortunately, the truth. O you with the black heart that found no way to apologize or make up or be amiable. After that no conversation took place between us other than about necessities and the household budget. Vengeance became mingled with the cost of living. The spring of compassion ran dry. As with a prisoner, my dreams revolved around escape. The desires of my heart dried up, and desolation closed over it. And all the while she behaved like a free woman, going and coming without permission or even letting me know. Silence enveloped her, and she uttered no word unless she had to. Pride encompassed her secret, and she complained of me to no one but my sister Siddiqa. When Siddiqa did not do what Seham expected, but sought to make peace between us, she hated her in turn. She said that it was not the madness of one man but a madness running in the family.

Seizing the opportunity of being alone with Samira and Gamal, I asked their opinion of what they had seen of our situation. "Your situation is not a happy one, Father," Gamal had said. "It's like the situation of our country, or even worse, and I'm planning to emigrate at the first opportunity."

I know his recalcitrance well, but as for Samira, she is a sensible girl, religious and modern at one and the same time, and yet she said, "I'm sorry, Father, but neither on your side nor on hers is there any tolerance."

"I was defending you, Samira."

"I wish you hadn't done so. She would have made it up with me after an hour, but you get angry so quickly, Father."

"But she's unreasonable."

"Our whole home is unreasonable."

"I chose you to be a judge."

"No, I'm in no way entitled to be that."

"I have found no comfort from either of you."

To which Gamal said, "We have no comfort for you or for ourselves."

If these two have not loved me as I have loved them, then what good do I wish for in this existence? Ah, look and enjoy, and move from place to place. As for the life that is being lost, live the moment that you are in and forget the past completely. Take your fill, for you will not see again that which you are leaving. Every moment is the last. From a world with which I am not satiated and whose pleasures I have not renounced, a world that has been snatched from me in a hasty outburst of anger. Which of these streets has not seen us together? Or has not seen our whole family, with Samira and Gamal going ahead of us? Was there no way of repairing the discord?

The cruelest punishment is having to bid farewell to Alexandria in the splendor of its white autumn—and in the prime of mature manhood. And here is the silent sea on the other side of Abu Qir, and together we sing, "O for the bliss you are in, my heart." In a dialogue of song between two watchful hearts. With Samira and Gamal breathlessly counting the number of fishing boats at anchor above the moon's sparkling reflections. Is a single day sufficient for making a tour of the landmarks of a quarter of a century? Why do we not record the sweet avowals at the time so that they may be of benefit to us in the hour of dryness? Memories are as numerous as the leaves of the trees, and the period of time remaining is as short as happiness. Happiness, when it presents itself, dispels awareness, and double-crosses us when it vanishes.

And who have I to bring me together with Dawlat? There is no possibility of that today. And were it possible it would only make matters worse and compromise me prematurely. And what is the point of pretending to a love that is nonexistent? Despair is what pushed me into it. She never stopped hinting at marriage, without caring about the fate of Samira and Gamal. It is not love but rather a whim of revenge. If only I had halted there and not crossed over to the fatal blow.

As evening falls, the search for me no doubt intensifies. So let me wait in Asteria, the place I love best of all for passing the evening. The meeting place of families, lovers, and rosy dreams. Beer and a light supper. Perhaps I shall be the only one by myself. Forgive me, Samira. Forgive me, Gamal. I had met the morning with a sincere and open heart, but anger hurls us into the path of perils. I entreated that the hour might be put back by just one minute. And when the violent tensions had vanished, nothing was left but despair with its icy, tongue-tied face. I undertook this farewell excursion with death sometimes following at my back, sometimes preceding me. Life has been abbreviated into hours, and I have understood life more than at any time past. How happy are the people around me, and were they to know my secret they would be happier still! Amiably, the waiter asks me, "Where's Madam?"

"She's out of town," I answer with hidden dejection.

There was no time left. Soon two or more men would approach me. "You are Mustafa Ibrahim?"

"Yes sir."

"Would you be good enough to come with us?"

I answer with total calm. "I was waiting for you."

By a Person Unknown

There was nothing unusual in the flat to attract attention, nothing that could be of any help to an investigator. It consisted of two rooms and an entrance hall, and in general was extremely simple. What was truly worthy of surprise was the fact that the bedroom should have remained in its natural state, retaining its normal tidiness despite the ghastly murder that had been committed there. Even the bed was undisturbed, or altered only to the extent that occurs when a bed has been slept in. However, the person lying on it was not asleep but had been murdered, the blood not yet dry. As evidenced by the mark of the cord around the neck and the protruding eyeballs, he had been strangled. Blood had coagulated around the nose and mouth, but apart from this there was no sign of any struggle or resistance in the bed, in the bedroom, or in the rest of the flat. Everything was normal, usual, familiar.

The officer in charge of the case stood aghast, his trained eyes searching out the corners, examining and noting, but achieving nothing. Without doubt he was standing before a crime, and there was no crime without a criminal, and the criminal could not be brought to light other than through some clue. Here all the windows were securely closed, so the murderer had come in and gone out by the door. Also, the murdered man had died of strangulation with a cord. How, then, had the murderer been able to wind the cord around the man's neck? Perhaps he had been able to do so while his victim was asleep. This was the acceptable explanation, there being no trace of any resistance. Another explanation was that he had taken his victim unawares from behind, done him in, laid him out on the bed, put everything back in order, and then gone off without leaving a trace. What a man! What nerves! He operated with patience, deliberation, calm, and precision, as happens only in fiction. In control of himself, of the murdered man, of the crime, and of the whole location—then off he goes, safe and sound! What a murderer!

In his mind the officer arranged the investigatory steps (the motive for the crime, the questioning of the concierge and the old servant woman), and also made a number of possible hypotheses. As much as he could he suppressed his strong emotions, then went back to thinking about the strange criminal who had crept into the flat, done away with a human being, and then gone off without a trace, like a delightful waft of breeze or shaft of sunlight. He searched the cupboard, the desk, and the clothes, and found a wallet containing ten pounds; he also came across the man's watch and a gold ring. It would seem that theft was not the motive for the crime. What, then, was the motive?

He asked for the concierge to be brought for questioning. He was an elderly Nubian who had worked in the small building on Barrad Street in Abbasiyya for many years. He made statements of some relevance. He said the murdered man had been a retired teacher named Hasan Wahbi. He was over seventy years of age and had lived alone ever since the death of his wife. He had a married daughter in Asyout and a son working as a doctor in Port Said. He himself was originally from Damietta and was being looked after by Umm Amina, who used to come at about ten in the morning and leave around five in the afternoon.

"And you, don't you sometimes perform services for him?"

"Not once in a year," said the old man quickly and emphatically. "I see him only at the door when he's going out and coming back."

"Tell me about yesterday."

"I saw him leaving the house at eight."

"He didn't ask you to clean the flat?"

With a certain asperity the man answered: "I've told you, not once in a year, not once in his lifetime. Umm Amina comes at ten to cook his food, clean the flat, and wash his clothes."

"Does she leave any windows open?"

"I don't know."

"Isn't it possible for someone to enter by the window?"

"As you can see, his flat is on the third floor, so it's not possible. Also, the building is faced on three sides by other buildings, while the fourth side overlooks Barrad Street itself."

"Go on with what you were saying."

"He left the house at eight, then returned at nine. This has been his usual routine every day for more than ten years. After that he stays in his flat until the next morning."

"Does no one visit him?"

"Except for his son and daughter, I don't remember seeing anyone visit him."

"When were they last here?"

"On the occasion of the feast of Greater Bairam."

"Doesn't the milkman or the paperman call?"

"The papers he brings back with him after going out in the morning. As for the yogurt, Umm Amina takes it in during the afternoon."

"Did she take it in yesterday?"

"Yes, I saw the boy going up to the flat and saw him leaving."

"When did Umm Amina leave the flat yesterday?"

"At about sunset."

"And when did she come today?"

"About ten. She rang the bell, and he didn't answer the door."

"Did he go out today as usual?"

"No, he didn't."

"Are you sure?"

"I didn't see him go out. I was sitting at my place by the door until Umm Amina arrived. Then, after a quarter of an hour, she returned to tell me he wasn't answering, so I went up with her. I rang the bell and knocked on the door, and when he didn't answer we went off to the police station. . . ."

The officer decided that this concierge was not capable of strangling a chicken, nor was Umm Amina, though they might make it possible for someone else to come in and go out. But why was Mr. Hasan Wahbi murdered? Was there some undiscovered theft? Had the wallet been left untouched for the purpose of putting the police off the scent? And was the presence of the key to the flat in the desk drawer another trick?

Umm Amina said she had been working in the schoolmaster's house for a quarter of a century—fifteen years during the lifetime of his wife and ten years following her death. The man had decided that she should spend the night at her own home ever since he had become a widower. She herself was a widow, she said, and the mother of six girls, all of whom were now married to workers or craftsmen; and she provided all their addresses.

"Yesterday he was in good health. He read through the newspapers, recited aloud a portion of the Koran, and when I left the flat, he was listening to the radio."

"What do you know of his family?"

"They are from Damietta, but he's hardly in touch with them and no one visits him except for his son and daughter at feast times and holidays."

"Do you know if he had any enemies?"

"None at all."

"No one used to visit him at home?"

"Never. Very rarely he would sit at the café on a Friday with some of his colleagues or former students."

The officer wondered how it was possible for the crime to have occurred without any motive or clues.

The necessary formalities were completed and, with the help of his assistant, the living quarters of the concierge were searched, as well as the homes of Umm Amina and her six daughters. Then the few friends of the deceased were summoned for examination, but not one of them gave evidence of any significance. The murder of the man appeared to be a complete and baffling mystery. The news of it spread through the street and later appeared in the papers, then the whole of Abbasiyya learned of it, and many people were saddened. The doctor, the murdered man's son, confirmed that his father possessed nothing of value and that his bank account had contained no more than the one hundred pounds he had saved in case of emergency and had in the end taken out. He also confirmed that the old man had had no enemies and that his murder might well have been from greed for some imaginary fortune the criminal had supposed him to have at his home. A thorough questioning of the concierge and Umm Amina took place and came to nothing, both of them being released without bail.

The investigating officer found himself in a fog of confusion and suffered from a sense of frustration he had not previously known. He had an honorable history in the fighting of crime, both in the towns and in the countryside, and was in general an officer with a high reputation. This was the first crime to defeat him so utterly and without his being accorded so much as a ray of hope or consolation. He sent off his scouts among the suspicious characters in the Muqattam Hills, on the borders of the district of Waili, and in Arab al-Mohammedi, but they all came back with nothing. The forensic doctor reported that Mr. Hasan Wahbi had died of strangulation, and he examined all his belongings in the hope of coming across a fingerprint or a hair or any clue that the criminal might have left behind him, but his efforts were in vain. Everyone found himself standing before a silent void.

Because of the severe defeat he had suffered, Officer Muhsin Abd al-Bari, who lived not far away, in a street that led to the police station, felt disconcerted, and his peace of mind was disturbed. When his wife noticed his depression, she said gently, "Don't get yourself into a state about it for nothing."

He retreated into silence and kept his mind off things by reading. He was fond of the mystical poets, such as Saadi, Ibn al-Farid, and Ibn al-Arabi, a rare enough hobby for a police investigation officer, and he therefore hid it even from his best friends.

The incident continued to be the talk of Abbasiyya, both because of its bewildering mystery and because the deceased had been the teacher of many of the young and middle-aged inhabitants of the district. But with the passing of a week or so the news became lost in the fearsome sea of oblivion, and even Muhsin Abd al-Bari entered it among the crimes committed by "person or persons unknown," saying to himself as he chewed over his bitter defeat, "Unknown! This one certainly is unknown!"

A month later the officer was called to an old mansion in the main street of Abbasiyya, the scene of a similar crime. It was as though the first crime had been repeated. Muhsin could hardly believe his eyes. The murdered man was a former army major general. He was living with his family, which consisted of a wife of sixty, a widowed sister also of sixty, and his youngest son, who was a twenty-year-old university student. Also living in the mansion were the concierge, the gardener, the chauffeur, the cook, and two other servants.

The major general was found one morning apparently asleep in bed as usual. It was, however, later than was normal, and it was this that had led his wife to come to see if he was all right.

But he had not been sleeping, he had been strangled, the mark of the cord scored around his neck, his eyes bulging horribly, and sticky blood around his mouth and nose. As for the room, it was undisturbed, even the bed itself, and no sound had been heard during the night to awaken any of his family, who slept on the same floor. The long and short of it was that the officer found himself once again facing the deadly mystery that had crushed him a month before at the home of the teacher Hasan Wahbi, facing too the person unknown, with his silence, his obscureness, his singular cruelty, his preposterous mockery.

"Was anything stolen?"

"No."

"Did he have any enemies?"

"None."

"And the servants, did he have a good relationship with them?"

"Very good."

"Do you have any suspicions about anyone?"

"None at all."

The officer went through the formalities without hope. He examined the mansion thoroughly and questioned the family and the servants. He had a sensation of fear of some person unknown, and felt that a plot was being hatched in the dark to do away not only with many victims, but also with his reputation and all the values in his life. He likewise felt that there was some sort of an enigma that was about to suffocate him with the weight of its mystery, and that if once again he were to fail, he would not be able to face up to life, that life itself would not be worthwhile for anyone.

Owing to the status of the murdered man, a number of senior investigation officers came to take charge of the case. "There's certainly been a crime," said one of them in astonishment, "but it's as though it has been committed without a criminal."

"But the criminal's there all right, and maybe he's closer to us than we imagine."

"How did he do it?"

"He passed a thin cord around the neck, pulling it tight until the man was dead. But how did he reach the site of his crime? How did he get away without leaving a trace?"

"And what's the motive for the killing?"

"Motives for killing are as numerous as those for living!"

"Could he kill for no reason?"

"If he were mad he would kill for no reason—or without such reason as would convince us."

"What's the connection between the major general and the teacher?"

"Both were susceptible to death!"

The news was printed on the front pages of the newspapers in sensational headlines. Public opinion was shaken, in particular among the inhabitants of Abbasiyya, for the major general had been known since the time of the elections, having put himself forward as a candidate on a number of occasions and having once been elected to the Senate. Muhsin mobilized all the detectives on the force to investigate and make inquiries. He issued them strict instructions and applied himself to his work with a feverish desire to succeed. At the end of the night, he returned home utterly fatigued in body and spirit. He resolved to keep his worries from his wife, who had at the time begun to suffer the discomforts of pregnancy. The thing he feared most was that he would be transferred from the police station of al-Waili, bearing the mark of disgrace at his defeat, and be replaced by someone else, just as he had replaced others in the countryside at the time of his victories and successes. He tried to rid himself of his worries by reading poetry, but in vain, for his mind fixed itself solely on the crime that had become for him the symbol of his defeat.

Who could this terrible killer be? He was not a thief, or someone seeking revenge, nor even a madman—a madman might kill, but he would not carry out his crime with such devastating perfection. He was confronted by a strong, overpowering riddle from whose wantonness there was no escape. How, then, was he to bear the responsibility of protecting lives?

People, especially those of Abbasiyya, lost interest in the subject and calmed down slightly. The officer's apprehension turned into a composed sadness harbored within the depths of his soul.

It was then that the third murder occurred. It happened forty days after the death of the major general. The location was a medium-sized house in Bain al-Ganayen, its victim a young woman in her thirties, the wife of a small contractor and the mother of three children. As usual everything was normal, other than the livid mark of the cord around the neck, the blood around the mouth and nose, and the bulging eyeballs. Apart from this there was no trace of anything. Muhsin carried out his routine duties in a quiet spirit of despair, for he believed that his torture would never come to an end and that he had been set up as a target by some merciless power. The mother of the murdered woman had lived with her. "In the morning I went in to find out how she was and I found her . . ." She was choked by tears and kept silent until the outburst of crying had passed. "The poor thing had typhoid ten years ago. . . ."

"Typhoid!" Muhsin called out in surprise at this irrelevant piece of information.

"Yes, her condition was serious, but she was not to die from it."

"You were not aware of any movement during the night?"

"None at all. The children were asleep in this room, while I slept on that sofa close by her room so as to be within earshot if she called. I was the last to go to sleep and the first to wake up. I went into her room and found her, poor love, as you can see. . . ."

The husband came at noon, having returned from Alexandria in a state of extreme grief. It was some time before he found himself in a state to answer the officer's questions, and he had nothing to say that could help the inquiry. He had been in Alexandria on business, having spent the previous day at the Commercial Café with some people whom he named, and he had spent the night with one of them in Qabbari, where he received the calamitous telegram. Giving a deep sigh, the man exclaimed, "Officer, this is unbearable—it's not the first time. Before this the teacher and the major general were killed. What are the police doing about it? People aren't killed without there being a murderer. You should be arresting him!"

"We're not magicians," burst out Muhsin, unable to endure such an attack. "Don't you understand?"

He quickly regretted his words. He returned to the police station, saying to himself that in actual fact it was he who was the criminal's number one victim. He wished that he could somehow declare his sense of impotence. This criminal was like the air, though even the air left some trace of itself in houses, or like heat, yet it too left its trace. How long would the crimes continue to have to be recorded among those committed by "a person unknown"?

Meanwhile Abbasiyya was in the throes of a terror that set the press ablaze. There was no other subject for conversation in the cafés than the stranglings and the terrible unknown perpetrator. It was a peril that had suddenly made its appearance, and no one was safe. There was no longer any confidence in the security forces, and suspicions were centered on perverts and madmen, this being the fashion in those days. From investigations it appeared that none of the inmates of the mental asylum had escaped. The police station received letters from anonymous informants, as a result of which many houses were searched, but no one of any importance was discovered; most of those involved were elderly. Somebody reported a young man known for being crazy or abnormal, who lived in Sarayat Street. He was arrested and taken off for questioning, but it was established that on the night the major general was killed he had been in detention in Ezbekiyya for importuning a girl in the street, so he was released. All efforts came to nothing, and Muhsin said sadly, "The sole accused in this case is myself!"

And so it was in his view and that of the residents of Abbasiyya, and that of the newspaper readers. Rumors spread without anyone knowing how they did so. It was said that the murderer was known to the security men but that they were covering up for him because he was closely related to an important personality. It was also said that there was in fact no murderer and no crime, but that it was all the result of an unknown and dangerous disease and that the laboratories of the Ministry of Health were working night and day to uncover its secret. Confusion and uneasiness reigned.

One day, a month or thereabouts after the murder of the woman, the policeman on duty at the al-Waili station found a corpse in the lane alongside it. Nothing like this had ever been heard of before. Officer Muhsin Abd al-Bari hurried to the place where the corpse lay—though it would have been possible to see it from the window of his room, had he so wanted. He found it to be the almost naked body of a man, certainly a beggar, lying against the wall of the police station. From sheer agony he almost let out a scream as his eyes alighted on the mark of the cord round the neck. Good Lord! Even this beggar! He searched the man, as though there might be a hope of coming across something. The local district official was summoned, and he identified the body as that of a mendicant from al-Wailiyya al-Sughra, a man of no fixed abode though known to many people.

The investigations took their course, not with any hope in view but as a cover to humiliating defeat. The residents of the houses close by were questioned, but what could be expected? Why not also ask those at the police station, which adjoined the scene of the crime? Detectives took themselves off to areas of suspicion, but they were searching for nothing in particular—for a specter, a spirit. As a reaction to the rancor that overwhelmed people's hearts, dozens of perverts and dubious characters were rounded up and detained, till the whole of Abbasiyya was cleared of them. But what was achieved? In addition, the number of policemen patrolling the streets was increased, particularly during the hours of night. The Ministry of the Interior allocated a thousand pounds as a reward for anyone leading the police to the mysterious killer. The press took up the matter in emotionally powerful tones on its front pages. All of this served to exacerbate the situation in the minds of the inhabitants of Abbasiyya until it was turned into a crisis of frightening proportions. Terror ruled as people's minds were tortured by evil presentiments, conversations turned into hysterical ravings, and those who could left the district. Were it not for the housing crisis and the circumstances under which people lived, Abbasiyya would have been emptied of its population.

Perhaps, though, no one suffered quite as much as Officer Muhsin Abd al-Bari or his unfortunate pregnant wife. By way of consolation and encouragement, she said, "You're not to blame, this is something beyond man's imagining."

"There's no longer any point to staying on in my job."

"Tell me how you've been at fault," she said anxiously.

"Wasted effort and being at fault are one and the same thing so long as lives are not safeguarded."

"In the end you will triumph as usual."

"I doubt it. This is something quite out of the ordinary."

He did not sleep that night. He remained awake with his thoughts, overwhelmed by a desire to escape into the world of his mystic poetry, where calm and eternal truth lay, where lights melted into the ultimate unity of existence, where there was solace from the trials of life, its failures, its manipulations. Was it not extraordinary that both the worshiper of truth and this bestial killer should belong to one and the same life? We die because we waste our lives in concerning ourselves with ridiculous things. There is no life for us and no escape except by directing ourselves to the truth alone.

Hardly had two weeks gone by than an incident no less strange than the previous one occurred. A body fell from the last car of Tram 22, in front of Street Ten late at night. The conductor stopped the tram and went toward where the sound had come from, and the driver followed him. They saw on the ground a man dressed in a suit—they thought he must be drunk or under the effect of drugs and that he had stumbled. The driver flashed his torch at him and immediately let out a scream and pointed at the man's neck. "Look!"

The conductor saw the well-known mark of the cord. They called out, and a number of police and plainclothesmen posted throughout the nooks and crannies of the vicinity hurried toward them. Two people who happened to be passing close by were arrested on the spot and taken to the police station. The incident caused a terrible shock, and Muhsin had to expend yet more hopeless and drastic efforts to no avail. One of those arrested was released (it turned out that he was an Army officer in civilian clothes), while several others were questioned without result. Muhsin tasted the bitterness of defeat and frustration for the fifth time, and it seemed to him that the criminal had none other than him in mind with his devilish pranks. The personality of the criminal made him think of mysterious characters in fiction, or of those creatures which in films descend to Earth from other planets.

Inwardly raging with his affliction, he said to his wife, "It's only sensible for you to go to your father's house at the Pyramids, far from all this atmosphere charged with terror and torment."

"Isn't it wrong for me to leave you in this state?" she protested.

Sighing, he said, "I just wish I could find some good reason for putting the blame on myself or one of my assistants."

The matter was discussed at length in the press and in detailed articles by psychologists and men of religion. As for Abbasiyya, it was seized by panic. At sundown it became depopulated, its cafés and streets empty: it was as though everyone was expecting his own turn to come. The crisis reached its peak when a child at the preparatory school for girls was found strangled in the lavatories.

Incidents followed one upon another in horrifying fashion. People were stunned. No one any longer paid attention to the tedious details about the examinations and inquiries being made, or to the opinions of the investigators as given to the press. All thoughts were directed to the impending danger that advanced heedless of anything, making no distinction between old and young, rich and poor, man and woman, healthy and sick, a home, a tram, or a street. A madman? An epidemic? A secret weapon? Some foolish fable? Gloom descended upon the semi-deserted district. Terror consumed it. People bolted their doors and windows. No one had any subject of conversation apart from death.

Muhsin Abd al-Bari roamed about the district like a man possessed, checking with the police and plainclothesmen, scrutinizing faces and places, wandering around in a state of utter despair, talking to himself about this despair and the pain of his defeat, wishing he could offer his neck to the murderer on condition that he would spare others from his devilish cord.

He visited the maternity hospital where his wife lay. He sat beside her bed for a while, gazing at her and the newborn child, relaxing his mouth into a smile for the first time recently. Then he kissed her on the forehead and left. He returned to the world in which he wished to be seen by no one. He felt something resembling vertigo. Life: terminated by the cord of some unknown person so that it becomes nothing. Yet without doubt it was something, and something of value: love and poetry and the newborn child; hopes whose beauty was limitless; being in life, merely being in life. Was there some error that had to be put right? And when to put it right? The feeling of vertigo intensified as when one suddenly awakes from a deep sleep.

Reports reached the station superintendent that it had been decided to transfer and replace Officer Muhsin Abd al-Bari. Extremely upset, the superintendent at once went to the room of the officer for whom he had such a high regard. He found him with his head flopped down on the desk as though asleep. He approached and softly called out, "Muhsin."

There was no answer. He called again, but the man still did not answer. He shook the officer to wake him, and the head tilted grotesquely. It was then that the superintendent spotted the drop of blood on the blotter. He looked at his colleague in terror and saw the mark of the infernal cord around his neck. The police station and its occupants were shattered.

A series of weighty meetings were held at the Governorate and urgent and important decisions were made. The director-general summoned all his assistants and told them in firm, rousing terms, "We shall declare unremitting war until the criminal is arrested." He thought momentarily and then went on. "There is something no less important than the apprehension of the criminal himself—it is to control the panic that has seized people."

"Yes sir."

"Life must go on as normal, people must go back to feeling that life is good." The questioning look in the probing eyes was answered by the director. "Not one word about this matter will be published in the press."

He discerned a certain listlessness in the men's eyes. "The fact is," he said, "that news disappears from the world once it disappears from the press." He scrutinized the faces. "No one will know anything, not even the people of Abbasiyya themselves."

Striking his desk with his fist, he declared, "No talking of death after today. Life must go on as usual, people must go back to feeling that life is good—and we shall not give up the investigation."

The Man and the Other Man

Out of the fruiterer's, carrying a conical screw of paper like those used for sugar, the man emerged. He was swallowed up in the vegetable market by a slow, battling stream of people. His smiling, ruddy face, his tall frame stood out, and the other man, from his position by the telephone booth, spotted him and said to himself, "At last—he'll not escape me."

He went on following the man closely until, slipping out of the crowd, he darted into the square. It was very important not to arouse his suspicions before the right opportunity presented itself. The man scanned the square till his glance came to rest on the confectionery shop on the opposite side; he made toward it around the right-hand half of the square, while the other man proceeded toward the same goal by way of the left-hand half. The man entered the shop, while the other stood under the tall lamppost.

The autumn weather was agreeably mild, the late afternoon light, gentle and falling out of a sky from which the disc of the sun had disappeared from sight behind a tall building. The man waited for the person serving to be free. His eyes ranged greedily along the rows of confectionery, Oriental and Western, and the other man watched him patiently.

A woman too was waiting; pretty, well dressed, she gave the unknown man an encouraging glance. The man regarded her with a look of curiosity. Half smiling, she turned away from him. He moved forward a step, invading her territory. Boldly, he whispered to her. They exchanged whispers. The other man told himself that this presaged a complication, a fresh addition to his troubles, an unexpected challenge to his plan. Her turn came to buy her requirements, then his. They exchanged a few laughing words, like the bubbles in honey. Then she passed into the street of cabarets. For an instant he followed her with his eyes, then walked off slowly, bearing the paper cone and the parcel. No doubt they had made a date, and the other hoped that this would not delay the carrying out of his plan; he hoped the long toil and skillful planning would not be in vain. The meeting might be soon, which would complicate matters; it could, though, be for a morrow that would never come.

The man set off. Walking did not seem to tire him. No one knew when his desires and greed would abate. As with a housewife, all shop windows attracted him. Watches, glasses, household utensils, clothes, spare parts, electronic gadgets, even medical accessories and the windows of chemists' shops drew his attention. He breathed in the smell of kebab and felafel; he read the titles of books and the names over bookshops. Whenever he was brought together with a woman or young girl he would enter her territory, but no fresh engagement of forces ensued. The hues of sunset took on a brownness, and the breeze exhaled a refreshing coolness. He entered a shop that sold cloth and came out carrying a nylon bag. He stuffed the package of confectionery into the bag, along with the cloth he had bought. He had also bought a book. What book could it be? When did he think he would be reading it? The other would have liked to know his secret interests. He scarcely knew anything of significance about the man except for his name and identity and his obscurely unpleasant history.

The man turned off into a shoeshine parlor. He seated himself on the revolving seat, placing what he was carrying on an old cane chair. Looking into the mirror in front of him, he ogled his face with admiring gratification; at times he stared straight at the image of himself, at other times he would twist his neck to right and left. Standing on the sidewalk, the other man watched him from an angle. For an instant their eyes met on the mirror's surface. Upset by this, the other moved a step forward, and the man disappeared from his line of vision. Now he could see nothing but the aged shoemaker and the corpulent woman who owned the place. The other man had been afraid his reflection would attract the man's attention, for his face was easily recognizable: swarthy, the eyes sharp, the hair black and thick. However, the man had been immersed in what he was doing and had not seen him. The streetlights came on and cast discreet evening shadows. Here he was, leaving the shop, even more pleased with himself now that he had had a shoeshine. A passerby in a hurry collided with him, and he moved back hastily, tightening his grip on the things he was carrying.

"Hey!" he shouted angrily.

The man in a hurry stopped in surprise but said nothing. Once again the man shouted at him. "You might at least apologize."

"Can't you be a bit more polite?" asked the passerby.

"No."

"Then I'll not apologize."

"You animal!"

The man in a hurry remonstrated by spitting on the ground, at which the man, placing his purchases on the pavement, fell upon him, and they exchanged vigorous blows. Realizing he was no match for his adversary, the man in a hurry fell back slightly, saying, "It's you who want to quarrel. See who started it!"

People collected, and a policeman came along. The other man observed all this, upset and irritated. When the policeman said that while the police station was handy and close it was better to settle things amicably, the two adversaries appeared to decide to avoid going to the station. And so, gathering up his belongings, the man went on his way. The other man, heaving a sigh of relief, followed him.

Faced by a toy shop, the man completely forgot his state of agitation. Did he have young sons? He went in. How persistent and persevering he was! He came out without having added to his purchases. Maybe he had bought nothing or maybe he had bought some large toy that the shop was going to deliver. At that moment he was confronted by a middle-aged man carrying a briefcase under his arm. They shook hands warmly and exchanged some hurried words. Then the middle-aged man went off, saying, "Don't forget the court case of the tenth."

Are you too someone who enjoyed indulging in lawsuits? When will you hear the judgment? I wonder where you'll be going after all this? A fruit juice—fair enough. You've tired me out, may God tire you.

For the second time their eyes met in a mirror. The other man's heart contracted. Did the man remember him? No, he was taken up with the taste of what he was drinking, and his eyes were watering. He looked but did not see as, with ingenuous admiration, he enjoyed the image of himself.

Leaving the shop and crossing the road, he disappeared into a tailor's to order a winter suit made. He reappeared after a quarter of an hour, turned toward the Freedom Café and went in. The café was on a corner and had more than one entrance, and the other man saw there was nothing for it but to go in too. He watched from where he sat, while not far away, the man sipped a cup of coffee and wrote a message. He gave the message to the waiter and got up to go to the telephone. He was now standing very close to the other man.

"Hallo. Hasan? Is the doctor there? . . . Make me an appointment as soon as possible. . . . Fine. Six P.M. Thanks."

Hardly had he returned to his seat than a friend joined him.

Sitting down next to him, the friend asked, "Did you go to the funeral?"

"Yes—I learned by chance."

"It comes to us all. Shall I ask for backgammon?"

"I don't have time."

"Just one game for a pound—win or lose."

The man looked at his watch and accepted the challenge. They played right away. At each throw of the dice, the man would make a sarcastic comment: he was an expert at psychological warfare, confident of victory. In less that ten minutes, he had risen to his feet and was stuffing the pound into his pocket. He went off laughing, with his adversary saying to him, "You robber—may God bless you with a pickpocket!"

The other man said to himself that this was a prayer that would most likely be answered.

Now the man made off toward the building where he lived, in the center of the city. This was the chance. It was not altogether guaranteed, and if it failed he would have to draw up another plan. Whenever one plan failed the plan that followed was exposed to fresh difficulties. There he was, disappearing into the entrance to the building. Catching up with him, the other man entered the elevator behind him. The two of them were alone. Without turning to him the man asked amicably, "Which floor?"

"The top."

"Me too."

But a woman reached the elevator before it moved off. The other man became frantic. When the woman left the elevator at the second floor, he regained his composure. This was the chance. Though the probabilities were many, the consequences did not worry him at all. With extreme care he grasped the knife that lay concealed in his pocket. . . .

He went out of the elevator. He met no one. Better than he

had foreseen, circumstances were working for him. He left the door of the elevator propped open, then hurried down the stairs. He made his way to the Ideal Bar, where he drank a lot and ate nothing but lettuce. He grew drowsy and dreamed a long dream in a very short space of time. Leaving the bar, he crossed in front of the building on the opposite pavement and saw the police and a great crowd of people. He continued walking to his hotel in al-Ataba. With a sigh of relief he entered his room, having totally forgotten his dream. He locked the door and put on the light.

Turning around, he saw the man sitting in the armchair, regarding him with a calmness that was as heavy as death. A deep groan escaped from him, and he retreated till his back was touching the wall. He sought desperately to flee but could not move. Nailed to where he stood, he urinated over himself. It was he for sure whom he saw, the man himself, in one hand the paper cone, in the other the bag: death staring out from a living picture, regarding him with motionless eyes that knew everything. He had a feeling of nausea, of dread, and told himself that he was either drunk or mad. Without uttering a word, the man ordered him to surrender; he was addressing him in a language that was new and clear, incisive yet inaudible. How and when had the man arrived with such speed? And what was the meaning of the police and the people gathered in front of the entrance to the building? How many years had gone by since he had committed his crime? How many years had he spent in the bar? With the passing of time, he became more sure about the man's presence, his weight and unbounded authority. Something prompted him to slip his hand into his pocket, and he came across the knife he had left thrust into the man's heart. It was then he realized that the world is subject to many laws, not just one.

Midnight struck. One o'clock. Receiving secret orders, he

meekly made ready to carry them out, scrupulously and with blind obedience. The man rose slowly to his feet and strode toward the door. He opened it, and the other man walked out in front of him, silent and obedient. He wanted to shriek, but the sound came to nothing in his throat. He went down the stairs, the man following him. On the way he met a houseboy, the hotel manager, the reception clerk, but no one heeded him. The miracle attracted no one's attention, caused no astonishment or interest.

In front of the hotel stood a carriage without a horse. The man moved toward the seat and quietly sat down. As for the other man, he took the place of the horse, putting the shafts under his arms. None of the passersby looked at what was happening. No crowd gathered. Every individual was occupied with something tangible or with something unseen. In fact one of the passersby even broke into song. "Those in love, O night."

At the crack of the whip, he began pulling the carriage. He went off gracefully, gently, submissively. He saw both sides of the road but not what stretched out ahead of him. Thus it was into the unknown that he plunged.

Moving forward in a straight line or making a turn, his instructions come to him through tugs on the reins. To where is the man driving him? What does he have in mind for him? He does not know and does not care. He goes on without stopping. He urinates and defecates without stopping. Sometimes he neighs and raises his head, touching the bit with his dry tongue, while the sound of his hoofs on the asphalt echoes rhythmically. A monotonous rhythm that gives warning of a journey without end.

The Wasteland

Let the battle be fierce and savage and let it satisfy the thirst for revenge that had burned through twenty years of patient waiting and watching. The man's face was aflame as his followers thronged behind him, some grasping their gnarled sticks, whose every knot gave warning of the breaking of bones, some carrying baskets filled with stones. The men proceeded along the desolate mountain path, vigorously resolved to fight.

You're in for a tough time, Shardaha!

From time to time a street sweeper or garbage collector would gaze at the strange procession, concentrating with a curious, probing disbelief on the man who occupied the central position. They asked each other about this tough whom no one had ever seen.

You will know him and remember him well, you scum.

The inclining sun cast scorching rays on the embroidered scarves, and a khamsin wind blew like a thing possessed, burning the men's faces and stirring up a loathsome gloom in the air. One of the followers leaned forward to the man's ear and asked, "Master Sharshara, does Shardaha lie on the mountain road?"

"No, we have to cross through the Gawwala quarter."

"News will spread quickly, and your enemy will make himself ready."

A frown came to Sharshara's face as he said, "What has to be done is not easy. A surprise attack will win the day, but it will not satisfy my thirst for revenge."

A thirst of twenty years' exile far from ever-wakeful Cairo, an exile spent in the darknesses of the port at Alexandria, with no hope in life but revenge. Food, drink, money, women, sky, earth, all were absorbed into heavy clouds; all sensation was confined to the aching state of being ever ready; the only thought to enter his mind was that of vengeance. No love, no stability, no leaving one's wealth untouched, for everything disappeared in preparing for the dread day. And so the bloom of life melted away in the furnace of rancor and painful hatred. You had no delight in your slow but sure ascendancy among the port laborers. You reaped no real benefit from your victory over the Gaafaris in the battles of Kom al-Dikka. Nothing was easier for you than to live as a revered and respected gang leader and to adopt Alexandria as your home and hear the name Sharshara ring out under its skies. Yet your bloodshot eyes saw nothing of the world but Shardaha, with its narrow road, its steep, rambling quarters, and its odious tyrant, Lahlouba. Curse him!

The desolate mountain track ended at the gateway. The procession of men passed through it into the teeming quarter of al-Gawwala. In a sharp, commanding voice, like the fall of an axe on stone, Sharshara called out, "Not a word to anyone."

The passersby made way for the procession; heads craned out of shops and windows and gazed at the unmistakable leader. Then fear and unrest spread.

"They'll think we've come to harm them," said Sharshara's companion, in warning.

Sharshara eyed the pale faces and said loudly, "Men, I give you safety."

Features relaxed and voices rose in greeting. Then, giving his companion a meaningful glance, he addressed the people, "We are on our way to Shardaha!"

He brandished his fearsome stick as he moved forward.

They are still looking at you in wonder. It is as though you had not been born in this quarter, in the very heart of Shardaha. But only murderers and criminals are remembered.

As a young man in his twenties, he had worked at the vegetable-oil press, his hobby playing marbles under the mulberry tree. He was an orphan who had no place to sleep except at the press, an act of charity on the part of Uncle Zahra, the owner. The first time he carried linseed oil to Lahlouba's house, he had been given a slap on the back of the neck—that was the way Lahlouba had greeted him.

And Zeinab, how beautiful she had been! Had it not been for Shardaha's tyrant, she would have been your wife these last twenty years. He could easily have asked for her hand before you did, but it seems she only became attractive to him the very night of your wedding. The hurricane lamps were broken, the singer fled, and the musical instruments were smashed. You were grabbed like some receptacle or piece of furniture. You were neither weak nor a coward, but to resist was beyond you. He threw you down under his feet, with dozens of other feet around you. He gave a hateful laugh and said scornfully, "Welcome, the linseed-oil bridegroom!" Your new galabeya was torn to shreds, your scarf lost, and what remained of your life's savings stolen. You said, "I'm from Shardaha, master. We're all your men and we rely on your protection."

He gave you a slap on the back of the neck, proclaiming his sympathy. He then addressed his men sarcastically. "What treatment, you vile creatures!"

"I'm at your service, Master, but let me go. . . ."

"Is the bride waiting for you?"

"Yes, boss, and I want my money. As for the galabeya, God will make it up to me."

Lahlouba grasped his forelock and dragged him along by it. "Sharshara!" he said in a new, frighteningly grave tone.

"Whatever you say, boss."

"Divorce her!"

"What?"

"I'm telling you, divorce her! Divorce your bride—now!"

"But . . ."

"She's beautiful—but life is more beautiful."

"I made the marriage contract with her this afternoon."

"You'll be writing the divorce document tonight—and the sooner the better."

He let out several groans of despair. Lahlouba kicked him mercilessly, and in seconds he was stripped of his torn clothes. He was thrown to the ground following a blow to the back of the head. Then he was beaten with a cane till he fainted, and his face was thrust into a hollow full of horse urine. "Divorce her!" Lahlouba kept saying.

He wept from the pain and the humiliating subjugation, but he did not protest. In mock sympathy Lahlouba told him, "No one will ask you to pay the sum agreed on in the event of divorce."

One of Lahlouba's men shook him violently. "Give praise to your Lord and thank your master."

The pain and the degradation and the lost bride. And now the perfumes issuing from the spice shop in al-Gawwala take you back to the past even more than has your actual return. The old places where you used to play, and Zeinab's face that you had loved ever since she was ten years old. Throughout the twenty years, your heart has moved only in rancor, while before that it had known only love and fun.

Soon I shall not grieve for the loss I have suffered in life. When I throw you to the ground at my feet, Lahlouba, and say,

"Divorce her," I shall take back the twenty years lost in hellfire. I shall find consolation for the money I have squandered on this gang of men, the money I had saved up through hard toil, theft, and risking my neck.

When the small tunnelway leading to Shardaha came into close view, he turned to his men and said, "Attack his followers but leave the man himself to me—and don't hurt anyone else."

He did not doubt that the news of his raid had preceded him to Shardaha, and that he would soon be standing face to face with Lahlouba. Nothing but a short tunnelway separated him from his objective. Warily he walked ahead of his men, but he met no one inside the tunnel. Then, all at once, they surged forward, raising their sticks, and letting out terrifying screams, but they found the street empty. The people had taken to their houses and shops, and Shardaha's street stretched away forlornly toward the wasteland that marked it off from the domain of desert.

Sharshara's companion whispered in his ear, "A ruse! It's a ruse, I swear by Abu'l-Abbas."*

"Lahlouba doesn't use tricks," said Sharshara in astonishment.

"Lahlouba!" he called out at the top of his voice. "Come out, you coward!"

But no one answered him and no one came out onto the street. He looked ahead of him in baffled expectancy and was met by a waft of chokingly hot dust. He was unloading a cargo of twenty years of anger and hatred. He saw the low arched door of the oil press; it was closed, and he advanced on it warily. He knocked with his stick until he heard a quaking voice imploring, "Safety!"

*A Muslim saint whose tomb is in Alexandria.

"Uncle Zahra!" shouted Sharshara triumphantly. "Come out, you're safe!"

The face of the old man appeared at an aperture in the wall above the door, and he cast a wary glance at Sharshara.

"Don't be frightened. No one intends you any harm. Don't you remember me, man?"

The old man looked at him for a long time, then asked helplessly, "May God protect you, who are you?"

"Have you forgotten your apprentice Sharshara?"

The clouded eyes widened, then he cried out, "Sharshara? By the Book of God, it's Sharshara himself!"

The old man quickly opened the door and hastened toward him, his arms open in outward welcome but inner fear. The two embraced. Sharshara refrained from asking his question till they had finished their greetings. "Where's Lahlouba?" he then asked. "What's wrong that he didn't come to defend his quarter?"

"Lahlouba!" The old man gulped, raising his head from a thin, emaciated neck. "Don't you know, my son?" he said. "Lahlouba died ages ago."

Sharshara gave a shout from the depths of his lungs, reeling under an unseen blow. "No!"

"It's the truth, my son."

Then in a stronger voice, a voice more terrible than before, "No. . . . No, you old dodderer!"

Taking a step back in fear, the old man said, "But he's well and truly dead, long ago."

Sharshara's arms slumped to his sides, and his whole frame seemed to collapse.

"It was five years ago or more," continued the old man.

Ah, why is it that all beings disappear and nothing is left but dust?

"Believe me, he died. He was invited to a banquet at his sister's house, and he ate some couscous and was poisoned, along with many of his followers. Not one of them survived."

Ah, he can barely breathe—it is as though the air has been turned into bricks. Sinking down into the depths of the earth, he does not know what remains of himself on its surface.

He stared at Zahra with heavy, lusterless eyes. "Then Lahlouba died?" he muttered.

"And the rest of his followers were scattered. It was easy for the people to drive them out."

"Not one of them is left?"

"Not one, thanks be to God."

Suddenly Sharshara shouted in a voice like thunder, "Lahlouba, you coward! Why did you have to go and die?!"

The old man was terrified at the violence in Sharshara's voice. "Take it easy," he beseeched, "and say 'There is no god but God.' "

Sharshara was about to turn to his companions with a gesture of resignation, but instead he asked listlessly, "And what do you know about Zeinab?"

In confusion the old man enquired, "Zeinab?"

"Old man, have you forgotten the bride they forced me to divorce on our wedding night?"

"Ah, yes. She sells eggs now in Donkey Lane."

Sharshara, defeated and broken in spirit, looked at his men, the gang on which he had spent his life's money. "Wait for me at the mountain," he said sullenly.

His gaze hardened as he looked in the direction of the men and watched them disappear into the tunnel one by one. Should he catch up with them? When and why should he do so? And should he return by way of Gawwala or via the wasteland? But what about Zeinab? Yes, Zeinab, for whose sake you burned up twenty years of your life. (Was it really for her sake?) You will not come to her over the body of a defeated tyrant as you had planned. He is dead, and there is no point in plundering tombs. How ghastly is a vacuum!

She is there in her shop. She, she herself. Who would have imagined a meeting so shamefaced, ambiguous, and lukewarm! He seated himself on a chair in a small café the size of a prison cell and went on observing the shop crammed with customers. There was a woman, a stranger, of plump proportions and wide experience, her homely features matured with the years. She was swathed in black from head to foot, but her face retained a fair measure of charm. She was bargaining and disputing, humoring and quarreling, like any market woman worth her salt. Here she is if I want her—and without a battle. Also without honor having been satisfied. Gone forever is the chance of standing over Lahlouba and ordering him to divorce her. How ghastly is a vacuum!

He did not turn his eyes from her for a single instant. Memories flowed through him strangely, sadly, and with a deadly bewilderment. He had no idea of what he would do now. He had firmly believed her to be his whole world—yet where was she?

Like the close of life, sunset descended. The customers went off one after the other. Finally she seated herself on a low rush chair and smoked a cigarette. As an escape from his confusion, he decided to present himself before her. He stood in front of her and said, "Good evening, lady."

In curiosity she raised two eyes penciled round with kohl. She did not recognize him, so she followed the smoke of her cigarette and muttered, "What can I do for you?"

"Nothing."

She looked at him again with a certain sudden interest, and

their eyes met in a fixed gaze. Her eyebrows rose, and the side of her mouth twisted into a half-smile.

"It's me."

"Sharshara!"

"The very same, but twenty years later."

"It's a long life."

"Like an illness."

"Praise God you're well. Where were you?"

"The big wide world."

"You've got a job and a family and children?"

"Not a thing."

"And at last you returned to Shardaha."

"A return of failure and frustration."

A doubting, questioning look gleamed in her eyes, and he said angrily, "Death beat me to it."

"Everything is over and done with," she muttered sadly.

"Hope was buried with him."

"Everything is over and done with."

They exchanged a long look; then he inquired, "And how are you?"

She pointed to the baskets of eggs. "As you can see—just fine."

"Didn't you . . . didn't you get married?"

"The boys and girls all grew up."

It was an answer that meant nothing. A feeble excuse that was like a snare. What was the good of returning before regaining one's lost honor? How ghastly is a vacuum! Pointing to an empty chair in a corner of the shop, she said, "Sit down." A soft intonation as in the days of old. Yet there was nothing left but dust.

"Another time." He hesitated in tortured confusion, then shook her by the hand and left. The time would not come again.

This is how you found yourself twenty years ago. Then, though, hope had not yet gone to its grave.

He hated the idea of going to the mountain by the Gawwala road. He did not want to see people or be seen by them. There was also the route through the wasteland, so it was toward the wasteland that he headed.

The Norwegian Rat

Fortunately we were not alone in this affliction. Mr. A.M., being the senior householder in the building, had invited us to a meeting in his flat for an exchange of opinions. There were not more than ten people present, including Mr. A.M., who, in addition to being the oldest among us, held the most senior position and was also the most well off. No one failed to show up—and how could they, seeing that it had to do with the rats and their likely invasion of our homes and their threat to our safety? Mr. A.M. began in a voice of great gravity with "As you all know . . ." and then set forth what the papers had been reiterating about the advance of the rats, their vast numbers, and the terrible destruction that would be wrought by them. Voices were raised around the room.

"What is being said is quite beyond belief."

"Have you seen the television coverage?"

"They're not ordinary rats; they're even attacking cats and people."

"Isn't it likely that things are a bit exaggerated?"

"No . . . no, the facts are beyond any exaggeration."

Then, calmly and with pride in being the chairman, Mr. A.M. said, "It has in any case been established that we are not alone. This has been confirmed to me by the Governor."

"It's good to hear that."

"So all we have to do is carry out instructions meticulously, both those that come directly through me and those that come by way of the authorities."

"And will this cost us a great deal?" it occurred to one of us to inquire.

He resorted to the Koran for a reply. " 'God does not charge a soul beyond its scope.' "

"The main thing is that the costs should not be excessive."

This time he resorted to a maxim. "An evil is not warded off by something worse."

At which more than one voice said, "We would hope that you will find us cooperative."

"We are with you," said Mr. A.M., "but do not rely upon us wholly. Rely too upon yourselves, starting at least with the obvious things."

"Absolutely so, but what are the obvious things?"

"Having traps and the traditional poisons."

"Fine."

"Having as many cats as possible in the stairwell and on the roofs. Also inside the flats if circumstances permit."

"But it's said that the Norwegian rat attacks cats."

"Cats are not without their use."

We returned to our homes in high spirits and with a sincere resolve. Soon, rats predominated over the rest of our worries. They made frequent appearances in our dreams, occupied the most time in our conversations, and came to engross us as life's main difficulty. We proceeded to take the precautions we had promised to, as we awaited the coming of the enemy. Some of us were saying that there was not long to go, while others said that one day we'd spot a rat darting past and that this would be the harbinger of imminent danger.

Many different explanations were given for the proliferation of rats. One opinion was that it was due to the Canal towns being empty after the evacuation, another attributed it to the negative aspects of the High Dam, others blamed it on the system of government, while many saw in it God's wrath at His servants for their refusal to accept His guidance. We expended laudable efforts in making rational preparations, about which no one was negligent. At a further meeting held at his home, the estimable Mr. A.M., may God preserve him, said, "I am happy with the preventive measures you have taken, and I am pleased to see the entrance to our building swarming with cats. Certainly there are those who complain about the expense of feeding them, but this is of little importance when we think of our safety and security." He scrutinized our faces with satisfaction, then asked, "What news of the traps?"

One of us (an eminent educator) answered. "I caught a skinny specimen—one of our local rats."

"Whatever a rat's identity, it's still harmful. Anyway, today I must inform you of the necessity, with the enemy at our gates, for being even more on your guard. Quantities of the new poison ground up in corn will be distributed to us. It is to be placed in vulnerable places such as the kitchen, though extreme care should be taken to protect children, poultry, and pets."

Everything happened just as the man said, and we told ourselves that we were truly not alone in the battle. Gratitude welled up in us for our solicitous neighbor and our revered Governor. Certainly all this had required of us a lot of care on top of our daily worries. And unavoidable mistakes did occur. Thus a cat was killed in one home and a number of chickens in another, but there were no losses in terms of human life. As time went on we became more and more tense and alert, and the suspense weighed heavily on us. We told ourselves that the happening of a calamity was preferable to the waiting for it. Then, one day, I met a neighbor at the bus stop, and he said, "I heard from a reliable source the rats have annihilated an entire village."

"There was not a thing about this in the papers!"

He gave me a scornful look and said nothing. I imagined the

earth heaving with hordes of rats as far as the eye could see and crowds of refugees wandering aimlessly in the desert. Good God, could such a thing come about? But what was so impossible about it? Had not God previously sent the Flood and the flocks of birds as mentioned in the Koran? Would people tomorrow cease their daily struggle and throw all they possessed into the raging fires of battle? And would they be victorious, or would this spell the end?

At the third meeting, Mr. A.M. appeared in cheerful mood. "Congratulations, gentlemen," he said. "We are as active as can be. The losses are slight and will not, one hopes, recur. We shall become experts in matters of fighting rats, and perhaps we shall be called upon in the future in other places. His Excellency the Governor is extremely happy."

One of our number began to complain. "The fact is that our nerves—."

But he was cut short by Mr. A.M. "Our nerves? Do you want to spoil our success with a thoughtless word?"

"When will the rats begin their attack?"

"No one can give a definite answer to that, and it is of no consequence so long as we are prepared for the battle." Then, after a pause, he continued. "Latest instructions are of special importance, relating as they do to windows, doors, and any apertures in walls or elsewhere. Close all doors and windows and examine in particular the lower part of any door. If any space is found through which a mere straw could pass, seal it up completely with wooden planks. When doing the morning cleaning, the windows of one room should be opened, and while one person sweeps, another, armed with a stick, should stand at the ready. Then you should close the windows and move to the next room, where the same procedure should be followed. On finishing the cleaning, the flat should be left like a firmly closed box, whatever the weather."

We exchanged looks in glum silence.

"It's impossible to go on like that," said a voice.

"No, you must maintain the utmost precision in carrying out . . ."

"Even in a prison cell there's . . ."

"We are at war, that is to say in a state of emergency. We are threatened not only with destruction but also with epidemics—God spare us. We must reckon with that."

We went on submissively carrying out what we had been ordered to do. We became more deeply submerged in a morass of anticipation and wariness, with the boredom and depression that accompany them. The nervous tension increased and was translated into sharp daily quarrels between the man of the house and his wife and children. We continued to follow the news, while the Norwegian rat, with its huge body, long whiskers, and alarming glassy look, became a star of evil that roamed in our imaginations and dreams and occupied the major part of our conversation.

At the last meeting, Mr. A.M. had said, "I've got some good news—a team of experts has been assigned to the task of checking the buildings, flats and locations exposed to risk, and all without any demand for additional rates."

It was indeed good news, and we received it with universal delight, the hope being that we would be able to relieve ourselves of some of the distress we had been suffering. Then one day the concierge informed us that a bureaucrat had inspected the entrance to the building, the stairwell, the roof, and the garage, and had pronounced favorably on the large bands of cats roaming about here and there. He had instructed the concierge to be extra vigilant and to inform him of any rat that might make its appearance, be it Norwegian or Egyptian.

One week after the meeting, the doorbell of our flat rang and the concierge gave us the good news that the bureaucrat was on his way and wished to have permission to make an inspection. The time was not convenient, because my wife had just finished preparing lunch, but I nevertheless hurried out to greet him. I found myself standing before a middle-aged, sturdily built man with a thick mustache, his square face with its short snub nose and glassy stare reminding me of a cat. I greeted him, concealing a smile that almost transformed itself into a laugh, and told myself that they really did have a flair for choosing their men. I walked ahead of him, and he proceeded to examine the traps and poisons, the windows and doors, nodding his head in approval. He did, however, find in the kitchen a small window covered over with a wire mesh of tiny holes, at which he said firmly, "Close the window."

My wife was on the point of protesting, but he snapped at her. "The Norwegian rat can gnaw through wire."

Satisfied that his order had been carried out, he sniffed at the smell of food, thus proclaiming his commendation. I therefore invited him to eat. "Only a mean man refuses generosity," he answered simply.

Immediately we prepared a table for him alone, telling him that we had already eaten. He sat down as though in his own home and began gobbling up the food without any restraint or shyness—and with quite extraordinary voracity. Out of politeness, we left him to it. However, after a while I thought it best to check on him in case he might be in need of something. I gave him another helping, and while doing so I became aware of a dramatic change in his appearance. It seemed that his face reminded me no longer of a cat but of a rat, in fact of the Norwegian rat itself. I returned to my wife with my head spinning. I did not tell her what I had noticed but asked her to be pleasant to him and make him welcome. She was away for a minute or two, then returned, pallid, and stared at me in stupefaction. "Did you see what he looks like when he eats?" she breathed.

I nodded, and she whispered, "It's quite amazing, unbelievable."

I indicated my agreement with a movement of my spinning head. It seems that our utter astonishment caused us to forget the passage of time, and we only came to when we heard his voice from the hallway calling joyfully, "May your house ever prosper!"

We rushed out, but he had reached the front door before us and had gone. All we glimpsed of him was his swaying back, then a swift about-face as he bade us farewell with a fleeting Norwegian smile. We stood behind the closed door looking at each other in bewilderment.

His Majesty

A son of the earth, a scion of weeds, he had been brought up and had grown and developed in the garden that had once surrounded the old square of al-Ataba. From the unknown he had sprouted, to be tended by filthy hands that fed him with a crust, clothed him in a galabeya and robbed him of his humanity. Then one day, when he had grown big and strong, a passerby pointed him out and said to his companion in a loud, laughing voice, "He looks just like the king!"

The king! He knew there was a king, and from a distance he had seen the king's mounted escort. What did the man mean? The pointing and the surprised glance occurred again. Did he really resemble the king? Can such a thing really happen? He hurried off and found a mirror at the entrance of a furniture shop in al-Azhar Street, and took a look at himself, to see the king. So this was the king! Neither the raggedness of the galabeya nor the filthy state of his face could mask his appearance.

Having washed his face and combed his hair, he began to go back and forth across the square. He obtained one success after another, being pointed out and prompting comments. He continued on, smiling proudly at his priceless appearance. With the passage of time he became known in the district as "His Majesty," "His August Majesty." People scoffingly explained the extraordinary likeness by the well-known promiscuity of the late king, father of the present one. Who was to know whether perhaps . . . ? Was it not conceivable that . . . ? Was it so out of the question that . . . ? Thus it was that scornful remarks attributed to him the honored blue blood of the Mohammed Ali dynasty. He himself knew nothing about either a father or a mother, so anything was possible. Found lying on the ground, naked or in a bundle, he had grown up in the arms of nature, like his earliest forebears in olden times.

He toyed with the surmises about his wonderful yet unknown origin, expecting from his likeness the greatest blessings. The fact was that his imposing appearance lessened for him the agony of being a vagrant and to a great extent spared him blows from the truncheons of the police. He was also the most generous of vagabonds, the most upright of pickpockets. "If one day you are exalted by good luck," his companions said to him, "don't forget us!"

He promised to do well by them and to protect them, and he became even more attached to his fantastic dreams. His fame eventually reached the police station. The detectives set off and came back to report, "The right height, appearance and complexion—it's a miracle."

The superintendent himself decided to have a look. Standing before the young man, he scrutinized him in stupefaction, and after dismissing him, the superintendent found himself thinking about him as a real problem. Was it possible to disregard him as some insignificant joke? Should he not be put under surveillance so that he could be arrested red-handed? Not certain either way, the superintendent thought it best to communicate the facts to one of his superiors at the Ministry of the Interior with whom he had a close relationship. Investigations were carried out. The highest security centers were thrown into confusion and came to regard the matter with the greatest seriousness. "The affair may reveal doubles as yet unknown to us, at which point we shall be asked, 'Where were you, gentlemen?' "

"What's to be done?"

The decision was made to apprehend the young man and place him in the Tor prison camp, as a danger to public security who had to be put away. In this manner the problem was disposed of, the minds of the police were put at rest, and Farouk the Second was almost forgotten.

The July Revolution came about, and hammer blows were struck at the *ancien régime*. A journalist wrote about someone resembling the deposed king lying forgotten in a prison camp, and the words brought about the young man's release. He returned to his life of vagrancy, this time without illusions, though he gave thanks to God for his freedom.

Certain magazines published his picture, and he achieved a fame he had never dreamed of. A film company decided to produce a film depicting the corruption that existed in the time before the Revolution, and the king was to appear in it in a marginal role behind the events. The young man was invited to audition for the part. His performance proved satisfactory owing to the simplicity of it, and he achieved a not inconsiderable reputation. Even so, the road to success was not opened to him, for he was not shown to possess any particular talent.

The authorities came to the conclusion that there were too many stories about the young man and that his picture was being published too often. And so a new problem arose, one that no one had taken into consideration. "Our people are good-hearted," it was said with farsightedness, "and it is not unlikely that there are some who are sympathetic toward the king in spite of his corruption, and the existence of this young man could be a spur to such sympathy. . . ."

"Then the publication of his picture should be forbidden."

"The most appropriate thing is for him to disappear completely."

The young man thought he had been born anew in order to meet a new age. The small role he had played in the film set his ambitions ablaze, and he expected boons and blessings with each day the sun came up. Whenever he felt the bitterness of impatience, he comforted himself with the thought that God had not created him with this appearance without some profound purpose. . . .

But without apparent reason, he disappeared: no one any longer saw him at his usual times and places. It seems that he disappeared for good.

Fear

During that period at the beginning of the century, the people of Farghana were the most wretched of human beings. Their alley lay between the Da'bas quarter on the one side and Halwagi on the other. The two quarters were at bitter odds, and there was ceaseless strife between them. The inhabitants of both quarters were known for their ferocity, roughness, and belligerence, their prime amusement being to play fast and loose with other people and with the law.

In the time of Gu'ran, the big boss of Halwagi, and of el-A'war, the big boss of Da'bas, the enmity between the two quarters became more intense, blood was spilled, and many were the battles that raged along the tracks and in the Muqattam Hills.

"What have we done wrong?" the people of Farghana asked themselves uneasily, "when we're neither from Da'bas nor from Halwagi?" Because no sooner had battle been joined than they would be seized by terror and hide away everything they owned—or themselves—behind locked doors. It was not unusual for the two adversaries to be locked in battle on Farghana soil, where the crow of destruction would caw, carts would be turned over, chains would be smashed, and screams would ring out. The innocent would suffer indiscriminately until life for the people of the alley became unbearable, their own losses far outstripping those of the contending parties; even the happy ones began to hate their existence.

Then one day they sought the assistance of the men of religion. These did their very best to get the two enemies to agree to spare Farghana the woes of their battles. It was a great day when they succeeded, and Farghana relaxed to a sense of peace. But what sort of peace? It cost them dearly in the way of good behavior, tact, and strict adherence to neutrality in their conduct, to the extent that fortunes were expended and honor demeaned. Whenever it became too much for them to bear and they were on the point of rebelling, they remembered the tragedies of the past and put up patiently with the suffering. Yet despite all this, they did enjoy a period of comparative peace not previously known.

This was the position until Na'ima, the daughter of Uncle Laithi, vendor of liver, appeared in the quarter.

When the old man's sight became so bad he was unable to distinguish between a one-millieme and a two-millieme piece, he used to take Na'ima with him to help him in his work, and this was at the time when she was ripe for marriage. She embarked on her business life wearing a galabeya that, while covering her from neck to ankle, showed off her well-proportioned figure to the best advantage. It casually clung to the budding parts of her body and accentuated her face, with its plump roundness and color of a ripe doum fruit, and the almond-shaped eyes the color of clear honey in whose glances there played the liveliness of youth naively responding to admiration. The eyes of the young men gazed at her with interest, and they were drawn, as flies to sugar, to the oven on the handcart where the liver was cooked.

It was not long before old Uncle Laithi had recited the Fatiha, the opening chapter of the Koran, with a young vendor of sweet potatoes named Hamli, as a seal of Na'ima's engagement to him. People waited for the wedding celebrations to be held, but when they were gathered one evening at the Mulberry Café—so named because it was sited under the branches of a mulberry tree—they read distress clearly written on the old man's wan face. The owner of the café asked him, "God protect us, Laithi—what is it?"

The old man replied with a sigh. "The unlucky man finds bones in liver!"

Heads turned to him from over their water pipes and glasses of cinnamon tea.

"Na'ima," he said with meaningful terseness.

"What about her? Has Hamli done something wrong?"

The man shook his turbaned head and said, "Hamli has nothing to do with my worries. I met el-A'war, the boss of Da'bas, and he greeted me with extraordinary friendliness—then he told me he wants to marry Na'ima."

Eyes sparkled with interest and disquiet, then the driver of a donkey cart asked, "And what did you say to him?"

"I was all confused. With great difficulty I told him I'd read the Fatiha for her with Hamli and he shouted, 'El-A'war himself comes to you and you talk to him of Hamli?' The fact of the matter is, I panicked."

"And then?"

The wrinkles of the old man's face filled with disgust. "Without knowing what I was doing I stretched out my hand and recited the Fatiha with him."

"And what about Hamli's Fatiha?"

"I met with him and confessed my dilemma. The good lad was unhappy, but he went off without saying anything."

The men exchanged looks in silence, and the vacuum was filled with the gurgling sounds of the water pipes. The café owner decided to soften the old man's pain and said magnanimously, "You're not to blame. Any one of us in your place would have behaved as you did. Say a prayer to the good Lord and take it easy."

"But the trouble doesn't stop there," said the old man, striking himself with his clenched fist.

"And can there be anything worse?" enquired the café owner in astonishment.

"Two hours after el-A'war's Fatiha, I found Gu'ran, the boss of Halwagi, in front of me."

"God save us! And what did he want?"

"Also Na'ima!"

The owner of the café brought the palms of his hands together, then raised his face to the ceiling of the café as though addressing himself to the heavens. The old man said, "He stood in my path like divine fate. I didn't know what to say or do. Then I found myself compelled to confess to him about el-A'war's Fatiha."

"May we all be preserved!"

"He said, 'You blind old driveler, I say Gu'ran and you tell me el-A'war?' The truth is that I panicked. Not knowing what I was doing, I held out my hand and recited the Fatiha!"

"And what about el-A'war's Fatiha?"

The old man, in a state of complete collapse, said, "That's just the trouble—so come to my rescue!"

They at once perceived that the trouble had a direct bearing on Farghana itself, and that once again their alley was threatened with destruction. They all cast about for some solution, until a blind Koran reciter spoke. "She can't marry the two of them, that's out of the question. And she can't marry one rather than the other, because that spells death." Then he removed his turban and scratched his head for a long time without coming up with any answers.

The lupine-seed seller had a suggestion. "Let her marry Hamli in secret."

Many answered him in a single voice. "Not Abu Zeid al-Hilali* himself could marry her now."

*A folk hero.

When too much thinking had wearied their heads in vain, the Koran reciter said, "Say a prayer with me: 'O Munificent Possessor of Mercies, save us from what we fear!' "

In the morning people found a strange commotion going on in an abandoned warehouse in the alley. There was a group of builders, carpenters, and laborers working with great determination in the warehouse, getting it ready for a new life. Over the entrance had been fixed a large notice reading FARGHANA POLICE STATION. Then along came some policemen with an officer, who took over the new place. People gathered in front of the police station, and an old policeman told them, "The Commandant is angry—the violence must cease."

Some said that God had answered their prayers, but their hearts were not put at rest. Everything around them convinced them that violence was stronger than the government. During their whole lives they had not seen a single policeman challenging one of the big bosses, whereas the bosses challenged the law every moment of the day and night. No one had forgotten how the superintendent of the Daher police station had one day sought the help of Halwagi's big boss, Gu'ran, against a Greek drug dealer who enjoyed the protection of the French government and was threatening to kill him. How then could this small police station, these few men, possibly put an end to violence?

The young officer with the two gold stars and the red braid came out and seated himself in a cane chair by the entrance to the police station, then sent a policeman to the Mulberry Café to bring him a narghile—a water pipe. He was around twenty-five years of age, slenderly built, and with coarse features; there was nothing remarkable about him apart from a large head with crinkly hair. He looked at the assembled crowd and said with a strange simplicity, "Othman al-Galali, your obedient servant. Don't be afraid, the government is with you."

The people ingratiated themselves with him by smiling doltishly, and nobody said a word. Taking up the flexible tube of the narghile, he continued. "It's a disgrace for men to live like women. Don't let anyone get the upper hand of you."

When he did not find a single indication of encouragement, he said with a certain sharpness that signaled his impatience, "And whoever shields a criminal I shall treat as a criminal."

Their eyes blinking in confusion, the people then dispersed one by one, all safely getting out of the way. The officer explored the quarter with some of his men. He made the rounds of Da'bas and Halwagi, and wherever he went he was followed by looks. From windows and cafés and nooks and crannies, he was the target for stares of timidity, derision, or resentment. He passed by el-A'war, who ignored him, and he passed by Gu'ran, who ignored him and then gave out a resounding laugh, and all the while Othman remained calm.

Everyone realized that he was parading the prestige of the government, and Gu'ran resolved to take him unawares with a decisive response. In the late afternoon of the same day, a bloody battle broke out between Halwagi and Da'bas on the open ground of the threshing floor, and the news of it spread like fire in the wood store. Laithi's weak heart trembled, and Farghana's joints turned to water. Many people advised the father to marry his daughter to Gu'ran, for he was after all the stronger of the two. It would be the lesser of two evils.

The following morning Othman made his appearance wearing a galabeya just like all the other inhabitants of the quarter. At first the people could not believe their eyes, but his identity was confirmed by his well-known voice. "For the benefit of those who were frightened by the uniform, I have taken it off. So now let the tough guys come to me if they are truly men."

He moved off from the police station alone, without allowing a single policeman to follow him. Instead he was followed by stupefied men, women, and young boys. He made his way to

Halwagi with a resolution not seen in anyone before him, until he was standing in front of the Hazel Café, where Gu'ran was to be found among his companions and followers. Othman said quietly, yet with a frowning face that clearly threatened, "Yesterday you challenged the government. Now here I am, alone amid you, demanding my share of being challenged, so let any real man among you step forward."

A young man named Inaba insolently wiggled his belly a few feet away from the officer, who turned suddenly and gave him a violent blow in the stomach, at which the man fell motionless to the ground. Everyone was stupefied at this unexpected show of courage, while the onlookers backed away. All eyes were fixed on Gu'ran, sitting squat-legged on a couch, enveloped in his cloak. For the first time Gu'ran looked into the face of the officer. "Without reason you attacked a companion of mine."

"He deserved to be taught some manners and I did so, and your turn will come right away," shouted Othman.

"You're young," said Gu'ran, his face disfigured with scars, "so, for the sake of your family, take yourself off."

"Get up if you're a man, and step forward."

Derisively Gu'ran made no movement. Othman took several steps toward him, and speedily Gu'ran's bodyguards grouped themselves in front of their master.

"Do I see you hiding behind a wall of cowards?" said the officer scornfully.

"Stand aside," Gu'ran called to his men.

They quickly dispersed, like pigeons after a shot has been fired. Gu'ran leaped up. He was of medium height, with a compact body and thick neck. "Where are your policemen?" he inquired.

To this the officer replied with fury. "I'll beat you the way you beat others. . . ." And with the suddenness of a thunderbolt he gave Gu'ran a humiliating slap. Gu'ran screamed out angrily and sprang at him, and the two became locked in mortal combat. This was an amazing moment, which to this day the quarter has not forgotten: it was like the storied battle between the elephant and the tiger. It was a battle decisive in the quarter's history, and it changed its course forever. Every tough in Gu'ran's bodyguard, and indeed among el-A'war's men too, read his fate in it.

Gu'ran, with all the savagery in his blood, wanted to squeeze the life out of Othman between his iron arms, but the officer relied upon his agility and quick punches, an art wholly unknown to Gu'ran. The officer's punches landed on his enemy's jaws, chest, stomach, and crooked nose, and Gu'ran screamed with crazed anger. "I'll be cursed if I don't drink your blood!"

The men, prevented by their traditions from participating in the battle, shouted, "Death . . . death to him, Master!"

Screams, shouts, and general clamor rose up. The whole quarter was assembled under the vaulted tunnel that divided Halwagi from Farghana. Na'ima stood there trembling with excitement, nervously clutching at her father's hand as she described to him what was happening, what his feeble eyes were unable to see for themselves.

Gu'ran's head spun with the blows that rained down on him. His movements grew slower, his arms sagged, and his eyes stared out unseeingly. "The monster has fallen to his knees," called out Na'ima joyfully.

He had indeed fallen. Bent double like a bear, with his head sunk into the dust, he then collapsed on his side. Dozens of cudgels were raised aloft, at which Othman, out of breath, called out, "You women!"

The men backed away in shame, while one of them shouted at him, "Soon they'll be reciting the Fatiha over your dead body."

Othman took to roaming the quarters in his ordinary galabeya and the strange legend that had grown around him saw to it that he was received with respect wherever he went. Whenever he came across a tough, big or small, he would block his way and demand that the man say, for everyone to hear, "I'm a woman." If there was any hesitation, he would hurl himself at the tough and flatten him to the ground. Every day would bring battles that the officer would enter boldly and emerge from victorious. Only a few months were to pass before the toughs departed from Da'bas and Halwagi, and no one was left but old men, women, and children, or those who went about with lowered eyes and had washed their hands of violence. The weak felt as if they had been born anew, and they looked at the officer with affection and esteem in their eyes.

Uncle Laithi grew sick, lost his sight completely, and took to his bed, and Na'ima wandered around on her own with the handcart of liver. As the days passed she became increasingly beautiful, aided by the reputation she had gained from el-A'war and Gu'ran having recently competed for her. The alley expected from one moment to the next that she would be betrothed to some suitable bridegroom. Then, one night, Handas, the lad at the café, whispered to those gathered there for the evening, "Have you seen how the officer looks at Na'ima?" No one had noticed anything, so he went on. "He devours her with his eyes."

Each one, from his own vantage point, proceeded to observe Na'ima. They perceived that she usually made her pitch with her handcart by the wall opposite the police station; that Othman would steal glances at her with noticeable interest, his eyes exploring the places of particular beauty in her face and body; and that when calling out her wares, the inflection of Na'ima's voice would be tinged with coquetry. In her sidelong glances and in every movement in her dealings there were feminine nuances directed at a man deserving of attention. As one of the café habitués, on a subsequent evening, said, "He devours her and she likes being devoured."

"And poor Uncle Laithi?" muttered the café owner.

"Who knows?" said the lupine-seed seller. "Perhaps the officer has asked the old man to be his father-in-law!"

"Nothing is too difficult for God," said the blind Koran reciter.

The others' eyes, though, bespoke the extent of their hopelessness. "He's stronger than Gu'ran and el-A'war together," said a young man, "and heaven help anyone who lets out so much as a squeak."

And Na'ima stood in the moonlight, checking through the day's takings and singing, "Before him I was a fool." But, desiring peace, the young men steered clear of her, saying that no girl sang like that unless she was in love.

Not many nights were to pass before Handas returned with news. "Everything has come to light—I saw the two of them yesterday at the Shubra wasteland . . ."

"Have a fear of God!" warned the owner of the café.

"She was standing—God be praised—in front of the cart, and the officer was eating the liver like a wild animal."

"It's quite natural," said the Koran reciter. "It happens to everyone."

"But at the Shubra wasteland!" exclaimed Handas. "Didn't you hear, sir? I called on God's mercy for poor Uncle Laithi."

Sadness penetrated to the depths of their hearts. Then the café owner said, "Her father's decrepit, but it's the honor of the whole quarter."

"The quarter itself is too decrepit to defend her honor," said the lupine-seed seller.

Shame turned their faces sullen, and they were astonished that this should come from the man who had bestowed peace upon them. The narghile and its tobacco had no taste for them. "And what's to be done?" asked the young man.

"Just say 'I'm a woman,' " said the blind Koran reciter.

Na'ima noticed the silence and contempt that enclosed her, and she began making up to this one and that, testing her doubts, but she encountered a wall of rancor. She was not afraid of being attacked, safe in the knowledge that the toughest of the toughs was to be found at his place outside the police station, but she suffered a lonely isolation. She kept her head raised proudly, yet the look in her honey-colored eyes was as a withered leaf, devoid of any spirit. At the slightest passing friction she would flare up in rage and be ready for a fight. She would curse and swear, and shout at her victim, "I'm more honorable than your mother." And all the while the officer would be seated in the cane chair, smoking his narghile and stretching out his legs halfway across the alley. His body had filled out, his stomach was paunchy, and there was a lofty look in his eyes. His ardor, though, had subsided, and it seemed that Na'ima herself no longer aroused his feelings. Those who, despite everything, had not forgotten the benefits he had brought, sighed and said, "What will be will be."

Na'ima now spent only the shortest time possible in the alley and would then wander far afield into different quarters and not return until night. Because she was always edgy and spoiling for a fight, her features had become stern and sullen, the look in her eyes frigid. She had become marked by a certain dullness which showed that old age was rushing toward her without mercy.

When that magic of hers that had turned the officer's head had faded—or so it appeared to curious eyes—there were whispers in the corners of the Mulberry Café. In the moments of silence the gurgling of the water pipes could be heard in the dying light of the alley like a succession of mocking laughs.

At the Bus Stop

The clouds gathered and grew denser like night descending, then the drizzle came down. The road was swept by a cold wind full of the aroma of humidity. The passersby quickened their pace, except for a group that had collected under the bus shelter. The ordinariness of the scene would almost have frozen it into inactivity, had it not been for a man who rushed headlong like a madman out of a side street and disappeared into another street opposite. Following on his heels was a group of men and youths who were shouting, "Thief . . . catch the thief!" The uproar gradually decreased then suddenly died out, with the drizzle continuing. The road emptied, or almost so; as for those gathered under the shelter, some were waiting for the bus while others had retreated there for fear of getting wet. The noise of the chase again revived, becoming louder as it grew closer. Then the pursuers came into view as the men laid hands on the thief, while around them the youths cheered with high-pitched voices. Halfway across the road, the thief tried to make his escape, so they took hold of him and fell upon him with slaps and kicks. Receiving such a violent beating, he resisted and struck out at random. The eyes of those standing under the shelter were firmly fixed on the battle.

"What a cruel beating they're giving him!"

"There'll be a crime worse than theft!"

"Look—there's a policeman standing at the entrance to a building, watching!"

"But he's turned his face away!"

The drizzle increased so that for a while it formed an uninterrupted sequence of silver-colored threads, then the rain fairly poured down. The road emptied of all but those fighting and those standing under the shelter. Exhausted, the men then stopped their exchange of blows with the thief and surrounded him; puffing and blowing, they exchanged inaudible words with him. Then, heedless of the rain, they became engrossed in a weighty discussion that no one could make out. Their clothes clinging to their bodies, they continued determinedly with their discussion, without paying the least attention to the rain. The thief's movements expressed the vehemence of his defense, but no one believed him. He waved his arms about as though he were making a speech, but his voice was drowned by the distance and the heavy downpour of rain. There was no doubt that he was delivering a speech and that the men were listening to him. Under the rain, they gazed mutely at him. The eyes of those standing under the shelter remained fixed on them.

"How is it that the policeman doesn't move?"

"That's what makes me think the incident might be a scene being shot for a film."

"But the beating was real enough!"

"And the discussion and the speech-making under the rain!"

Something unusual attracted their gaze. From the direction of the square, two cars rushed out at a crazy speed. It appeared to be a furious chase. The car in front was tearing along, with the other on the point of catching up to it. Then the one in front braked so suddenly that it skidded on the surface of the road and the other knocked into it with a resounding crash. Both cars overturned, causing an explosion, and they immediately caught fire. Screams and groans rang out under the pouring rain. But no one hurried toward the accident: the thief did not stop declaiming, and none of those surrounding him turned toward the remnants of the two cars that had been destroyed a few meters away from them. They took no notice, just as they took no notice of the rain. Those standing under the shelter caught sight of a person covered in blood, one of the victims of the accident, crawling exceedingly slowly from under one of the cars. Attempting to raise himself on all fours, he took a final tumble onto his face.

"A real disaster, no doubt about it!"

"The policeman doesn't want to budge!"

"There must be a telephone nearby."

But no one moved, all fearful of the rain. It was a frightening downpour, and there were cracks of thunder. The thief, having completed his speech, stood regarding his listeners with calm confidence. Suddenly he began to take off his clothes till he was completely naked. He threw his clothes onto the wreckage of the two cars, whose fires had been put out by the rain. He walked around as though showing off his naked body. He took two steps forward, then two steps back and began to dance with a professional refinement of movement. At this those who had been chasing him clapped in time, while the young men linked arms and began circling around him. Perplexed, those standing under the shelter held their breath.

"If it's not a scene being filmed, then it's madness!"

"Without doubt a scene being shot for a film, and the policeman's merely one of them waiting to perform his part."

"And the car accident?"

"Technical skill—and at the end we'll find the director behind a window."

A window in a building opposite the shelter was opened, making a noise that drew attention to it. Despite the clapping and the downpour of rain, eyes were directed at it. A fully dressed man appeared at the window. He gave a whistle, and immediately another window in the same building was opened and a woman appeared, fully dressed and made up, who answered the whistle with a nod of her head. The two of them disappeared from the gaze of those standing under the shelter; after a while the two left the building together. Heedless of the rain, they walked out arm in arm. They stood by the wrecked cars, exchanged a word, and began taking off their clothes until they were completely naked under the rain. The woman threw herself down on the ground, letting her head fall on the corpse of the dead man, which was lying facedown. The man knelt alongside her and began, with hands and lips, making tender love. Then the man covered her with his body, and they began copulating. The dancing and the clapping, and the young men moving in a circle, and the downpour of the rain, continued uninterrupted.

"Scandalous!"

"If it's a scene in a film it's scandalous, and if it's for real it's madness."

"The policeman is lighting a cigarette."

The semiempty street then saw new life. From the south came a camel caravan, preceded by a caravan leader and several Bedouin men and women. They encamped at a short distance from the circle of the dancing thief. The camels were tied to the walls of the houses, and tents were erected, after which the people dispersed, some of them partaking of food or sipping tea or smoking, while others engaged in conversation. From the north came a group of tourist buses carrying Europeans. They came to a stop behind the thief's circle, then the passengers, men and women, got out and dispersed in groups, eagerly exploring the place, heedless of the dancing, the copulating, death, or the rain.

Then a lot of building workers came along, followed by trucks loaded with stones, cement, and construction equipment. With incredible speed the workers set up a magnificent tomb. Close by it they made out of the stones a large elevated throne and covered it with sheets and decorated its supports with flowers—all this under the rain. They went to the wreckage of the two cars and took out the corpses, the heads smashed in and the limbs burned. The body of the man lying on his face they also took from under the two lovers, who had not ceased their copulating. They ranged the bodies on the throne alongside one another, then turned their attention to the two lovers and carried them off together, still entwined, and deposited them in the tomb, blocking up the opening and leveling off the earth. After that, cheering with words that no one could make out, they boarded the trucks, which took them off with lightning speed.

"It's as though we're in a dream!"

"A frightening dream—we'd better be off."

"No, we must wait."

"Wait for what?"

"The happy ending."

"Happy?"

"Or else tell the producer he's got a catastrophe on his hands!"

While they were conversing, a man wearing judge's robes sat down cross-legged on the tomb. No one saw where he had come from: whether from among the European tourists, from among the Bedouin, or from the dance circle. He spread a newspaper before him and began reading out an item as though pronouncing sentence. No one could hear what he was saying, for it was drowned by the clapping, the clamor of voices in all sorts of languages, and the rain. But his inaudible words were not lost, for movements of violent conflict like clamorous waves spread along the road, with battles breaking out in the midst of the Bedouin, and others in the areas where the Europeans were to be found. Battles then started up between the Bedouin and the Europeans. Other people began dancing and singing. Many gathered around the tomb and began copulating in the nude.

The thief danced in a frenzy of singular invention. Everything became more intense and attained a peak: killing and dancing and copulation and death, the thunder and the rain.

A large man slipped in among the people standing under the shelter. Bareheaded, he was wearing trousers and a black pull-over, and he carried a telescope. He violently cleaved his way through the group and began watching the road through his telescope, moving it around in different directions and muttering, "Not bad . . . not bad."

The eyes of the group fastened on him.

"Is it him?"

"Yes, he's the director."

The man once again addressed the road, murmuring, "Keep going, don't make any mistakes or we'll have to take everything from the beginning."

Then one of the men asked him, "Sir, would you be . . . ?"

But he cut him short with an abrupt, unfriendly gesture, so the man swallowed the remainder of his question and kept quiet. But someone else, deriving courage from the tautness of his nerves, asked, "Are you the director?"

The man did not turn to his questioner but continued his surveillance, at which a human head rolled toward the bus stop, coming to rest several feet away, blood spouting profusely from where it had been severed from the neck. The people under the shelter screamed in terror, while the man with the telescope stared for some time at the head, then mumbled, "Well done . . . well done!"

"But it's a real head and real blood!" a man shouted at him.

The man directed his telescope toward a man and a woman copulating, then called out impatiently, "Change position—take care it doesn't get boring!"

"But it's a real head!" the other man shouted at him. "Please explain to us what it's all about."

"Just one word from you would be enough for us to know who you are and who these people are," said another man.

"Nothing's stopping you from speaking," implored a third person.

"Sir," a fourth entreated, "don't begrudge us peace of mind."

But the man with the telescope gave a sudden leap backward, as though to hide himself behind them. His arrogance melted away in a searching look; his haughtiness disappeared. It was as though he had become old or been shattered by some illness. The people gathered under the shelter saw a group of official-looking men wandering about not far away, like dogs sniffing around. The man tore off at a mad run under the rain; one of the men wandering around darted after him, followed, like a hurricane, by the others. Soon they had all disappeared from view, leaving the road to murder, copulation, dancing, and the rain.

"Good heavens! It wasn't the director after all."

"Who is he, then?"

"Perhaps he's a thief."

"Or an escaped lunatic."

"Or perhaps he and his pursuers belong to a scene in the film."

"These are real events and have nothing to do with acting."

"But acting is the sole premise that makes them somewhat acceptable."

"There's no point in concocting premises."

"Then what's your explanation for it?"

"It's reality, quite regardless of . . ."

"How can it be happening?"

"It is happening."

"We must be off at any price."

"We shall be called to give evidence at the inquiry."

"There's some hope left. . . ."

The man who said this advanced toward the policeman and shouted, "Sergeant . . . !"

He called four times before the policeman took note. He scowled, clearing his throat, at which the other gestured to him in appeal, saying, "Please, Sergeant . . ."

The sergeant looked at the rain in displeasure, then fastened his overcoat around his body and hurried toward them until he was standing under the shelter. He scrutinized them sternly and inquired, "What's it to do with you?"

"Haven't you seen what's happening in the street?"

Without averting his eyes, he said, "Everyone at the bus stop has taken his bus except for you. What are you up to?"

"Look at that human head."

"Where are your identity cards?"

He examined their cards as he gave a cruel, ironic smile. "What's behind your assembling here?"

They exchanged glances proclaiming their innocence, and one of them said, "Not one of us knows any of the others."

"A lie that will not help you now."

He took two steps back. Aiming his gun at them, he fired quickly and accurately. One after the other they fell lifelessly to the ground. Their bodies were sprawled under the shelter, the heads cushioned on the sidewalk under the rain.

A Fugitive from Justice

"The German army has invaded Polish territory. . . ."

The news burst forth from the radio jammed in an aperture in the wall of the sole room still standing in the ruins, and made its way beyond the boundaries of the vast Khafeer area.

"Quiet!" shouted Dahroug sharply. "Listen, the lot of you!"

The boy and his three sisters stopped making a noise. When they saw from their father's face that he was serious, they slunk off between the piles of scrap iron, tires, and spare parts to the most distant part of the ruins. There they continued their games, safe from his wrath.

Amna, hanging out the washing, paused and raised her head above the line stretched between a bar in the window of the room and the roof of an old truck. "You scared away the children," she called out at her husband in protest. "That blasted radio and its news!"

Dahroug, without anger, ignored her. He took a last puff from the cigarette butt he held between his fingers. "It's war, then!" he said.

Salama realized the words were directed at him, so he raised his head from the tire he had been fixing. With eyes gleaming out of a face surrounded by a thick black beard that reached down his neck, the man stared back, then said scornfully, "Yes, they finally believed it."

While Dahroug's head was turned toward the radio, Salama seized the chance to steal a glance at the woman. His gaze lingered on her face that craned upward, then descended to her slim body with the full breasts. The woman caught sight of him before he withdrew his stare, as though she had expected it. Then she turned her back on him, and Salama leaned over the wheel, thinking how terrible was war in the heat of August. How terrible the heat!

Dahroug turned toward him. "For a long time they've been predicting it will bring the world to ruin. But what's it to us?"

"We're far away," answered the bearded man, smiling. "Let them devour one another."

Dahroug crossed his legs as he sat on an upturned can and cast a dreamy look far afield. "We heard fantastic things about the last war," he said.

"The fact is you're old," said Amna, laughing.

Dahroug gave a laugh through his blackened teeth, saying scornfully, "All you care about is your stomach."

Salama, who though no longer young was a good ten years younger than his companion, said, "Yes, we certainly heard some fantastic things."

"Look at al-Asyouti for instance, who was he? Before the war he was nothing but a porter."

The children, having forgotten the threats, returned and brought with them their rowdiness. Mahmoud, a boy of seven and the eldest, was running about with the young girls trailing after him. His father glanced at him admiringly and called out, "Mahmoud, my boy, take courage—war's broken out."

In the late afternoon Dahroug and Salama sat together on a piece of sacking outside the fence around the ruins. Before them stretched the desert right up to the foot of the Muqattam Hills, the sands extinguished under their shadow. A faded yellowness, the remnants of choked breaths of high summer, was diffused into the limpid sky. Feeble rays from the inclining sun were quickly scaling the mountain summit, though the desert was puffing out a refreshing breeze with the approach of evening.

Dahroug began counting out piasters, while Salama, his head

resting against the fence, gazed distractedly toward the horizon. Amna brought tea, and the children, barefoot and half naked, ran to the wasteland. Dahroug sipped a little of the hot tea.

"My heart tells me, Salama, that the work's going to really take off."

"May your heart be right, Abu Mahmoud."*

"I wish I could rely on you."

"I'm your friend and indebted to you for your generous kindness, but I can't leave the ruins."

Dahroug thought for a while, then asked, "Does anyone in the big city know you behind that beard?"

"They know the very djinn themselves."

"And will you spend your life in the ruins?"

"Better than the hangman's noose, Abu Mahmoud."

Dahroug laughed loud and said, "I have to laugh whenever I remember the story of your escape from between two guards."

"The best way of escaping is when it's not expected."

Amna was standing facing the wasteland, her shawl drawn back over half of her jet black hair. "And the man got bumped off without any blood money."

"He was a murderer, the son of a murderer," said Salama angrily. "He was so old I was afraid death would get to him before I did. My family went on demanding I that take revenge."

Dahroug guffawed loudly. "And you made your escape when the papers were on their way to the Mufti to endorse the death sentence."

Salama tugged at his arm in gratitude. "And I found myself desperate and said, 'I've got no one but Dahroug, my childhood friend,' and you gave me shelter, you noblest of men."

*I.e., father of Mahmoud, Mahmoud being Dahroug's eldest son—a respectful and friendly way of addressing a man.

"We're men of honor, Salama."

"In any case the storehouse here is in need of a man—and I'm that man."

Their conversation was interrupted by the appearance of a funeral procession on the horizon. It was coming from where the buildings stood and it continued toward the road opposite the western fence of the ruins that led to the Khafeer cemetery. The coffin, shrouded with a white silk covering, came into view. "A young girl," muttered Amna. "How sad!"

"This place is beautiful and safe," said Salama. "The only thing wrong with it is it's on the road to the cemetery."

"Isn't it the road we all take?" said Dahroug, laughing.

The wasteland had remained substantially unchanged since war was declared. It was a playground for the sun from its rising to its setting, a place of passage for coffins, and an encampment for silence. The sirens were sounded in exercise for imaginary air raids. The old battered radio achieved the height of importance when it allowed Dahroug to calculate the shells exchanged between the Siegfried and Maginot Lines.

Whenever Salama's senses registered the tones of Amna's melodious voice, or a playful movement or glance, even if not intentional, he became aflame with a voracious fire and at the same time with a merciless anger against himself.

"Things haven't changed," said Dahroug morosely. "Where's all we heard about the war?"

"Be patient. Don't you remember what your Jewish commission agent said?"

Dahroug looked toward the piles of iron with which, acting on the advice of his agent, he had filled up the place. "Let the days pass quickly."

"Let them pass quickly—and let them swallow up fifteen years."

"Fifteen years?"

"Then my sentence becomes null and void."

"What a lifetime! By then we'll be on the brink of a third war."

Salama began singing in a strange, hoarse voice, "Come tell me, Bahiyya." Then he called out, "Master Dahroug, none of my family will be left but the women."

He told himself that Amna, without knowing it—or perhaps knowing it—was turning his head and that he would be going through hell before death took him. The war did not concern him in the least, but in between musical intervals on the radio he heard the news of Holland and of Belgium being overrun, and of the fall of Paris. In front of his eyes there passed the successive columns of refugees, and the void was filled with sighs and tears. Then Italy declared war. "It's knocking at the gates," said Dahroug uneasily.

But Salama was indifferent. "For us it's neither here nor there."

"The good Lord will look after us," muttered Amna as her gaze followed the naked children playing around a barrel filled with water.

For the first time the siren sounded for a real air raid. Dahroug and his family awoke, as did Salama, bedded down in the truck. Amna was frightened for the children and said that the shelter was too far away.

"Stay in the room," said Dahroug. "They won't bomb the wasteland or the cemetery."

Salama raised his head toward the full moon which stared down at them, eternally calm. "I see nothing but crazy lights," he said.

From the truck window he directed his gaze at the closed room. It stood against the fence to the left of the entrance, with a roof that sloped toward the door, and a colorless wall. The wall was daubed with moonlight; the room enclosed within itself hearts filled with apprehension. It was like some abandoned hut, and he imagined it veiled the night and the ruins.

The raid plunges down at the city and destroys all that exists in it: it topples the law, the Mufti, the judge, the warder, and the hangman's noose. The innermost parts of the earth burst open, and it sweeps everything aside. Even noble-mindedness has its breathing choked. From out of the debris there rises a naked man and a woman with clothes ripped apart; the wardens have been killed.

Night after night the raids followed in close succession, raids that were either as silent as the wasteland or interspersed with antiaircraft fire. Dahrough would go to Salama in the truck to look up at the sky and talk.

"The raids aren't as we heard."

"The Italians aren't like the Germans."

Dahroug laughed and clamped his hand on Salama's beard. "You're cheating the angel of death by going on living."

"Yes, I should have been in the grave at least a year and a half ago."

"Is that why you don't fear death?"

"No, I've feared it ever since I sniffed the smell of it as they carried me off to the Mufti."

"Just imagine what you'd look like now!"

"I give thanks to God who has spared me that I might see the searchlights and the antiaircraft guns."

A new energy pervaded the ruins, then things advanced apace in a manner undreamt of by Dahroug. Every day he would spend several hours away from the place. Later his business outside took up the whole of his day. Salama meanwhile worked diligently in the ruins as watchman and warehouseman. In his leisure time he would sit on a rubber tire with his back resting against the bumper of a truck, smoking a cigarette or combing through his beard, his sharp eyes yielding to an increasing compliance with his unruly desires. He told himself that she was ignoring his stares but that she was acutely conscious of them all the time and that his piercing gaze dominated her every movement as though manipulating some unseen thread. He looked at the sky and followed a kite as it made its farewell patrol at early evening, then looked down and saw her standing a few meters away in the direction of the tap from which water was flowing into a jerry can. "It's been a very hot day," he said.

She nodded her head in agreement and looked into his staring eyes, then lowered her head and hid a smile. The smile swept away the impediment of generosity of spirit in his breast, and he was carried off by a tornado of emotions. He gave an audible sigh, and the woman scolded Mahmoud, who, at the door, had pulled his sister by her pigtail. "Shall I make you tea?" she asked Salama.

"It's likely that he'll travel shortly to Sharqiyya province," he said in a tone rebelling against his control.

With evening Dahroug returned. He appeared tired and begrimed, but the gleam of success shone in his eyes. He laughed loudly as he said to Salama, "Man, war's not as they say. War's a real blessing." And he gave Amna a large parcel of meat, saying, "Hurry up—I haven't had a bite all day."

As he was changing his clothes in the room, his voice could be heard outside. "Tomorrow I'll be traveling to Sharqiyya."

He was away for two days. Late in the afternoon of the third day, Salama waited for him, seated on the piece of sacking outside the fence. Quiet and heavy lidded he sat, running his fingers through his beard, counting the kites that were still to be seen, and looking out at the wasteland with languorous self-surrender. From inside he heard Amna as she scolded the children in a voice vibrant with a sense of well-being, and he gazed at the sun's hem as it began to disappear suddenly behind the crest of the mountain. Night would soon descend. A noise from the west caught his attention, and he saw a taxi approach and draw up at the far end of the fence. Dahroug got out of it. He approached, striking the ground with firm, heavy tread, his head held high. Getting to his feet, Salama greeted him, and the two men shook hands, then Dahrough gave the other a punch in the chest and said, "Salama, you son of a bitch, the English are real men."

Salama gave him an inquiring look, and Dahroug continued boastfully, "They must be from Upper Egypt!"

Salama called on God to grant Dahroug continued success, and the man entered the ruins, calling out gleefully like a child, "Mahmoud, my boy . . . !" Then he began singing, "Give my greetings," and he snapped his fingers and danced.

Before dawn the siren wailed, and Dahroug and Salama went out to the wasteland beyond the fence as they had taken to doing of late. "The siren no longer frightens anyone," said Dahroug.

The desert flowed away under the moonlight, fertile ground for dreams. Dahroug gave a long laugh, and when Salama asked him what he was laughing about, he motioned with his elbow to the room. "Tonight saw your old Uncle Dahroug as he used to be during the nights of his youth."

A short silence descended, roofed by searchlights, then again Dahroug spoke in a tone that was both serious and brotherly. "Salama, today's not like yesterday. A lot of new clients will be coming, and I'm frightened for you."

"Must I go away?" asked Salama dejectedly.

"Yes, I'll smuggle you out to Palestine, and you'll work there for me. How do you feel about that?"

"Whatever you think best."

"Everything's planned and decreed, you son of a bitch."

Suddenly the earth shook with the convulsive reverberation

of an explosion that paralyzed their heartbeats. Dahroug pulled nervously at Salama's arm. "What's that?"

Salama, his face pallid in the moonlight, answered, "A bomb. Hurry to the room."

Amna's screams rang out, and Dahroug called to her, "Stay where you are . . . stay where you are, Amna."

The bombing continued without interruption. The two men ran toward the ruins. The next instant Dahroug gave a scream, then fell forward to the ground.

"Master!" shouted Salama. He leaned over to help the man to his feet, but he could do nothing. Then, helpless, he found himself being flung on top of him, his forehead sinking into the sand. The earth collapsed around him and the desert rose up toward the sky. Something opaque blotted out the face of the moon.

"What's wrong with you, Dahroug?"

A voice called, then the darkness swallowed up all sound and color. Salama wanted to say to his companion: "Forgive me—I am overcome by sleep."

But he uttered not a single word.

A Long-Term Plan

Yesterday the challenges were hunger and utter destitution; today the challenge is excessive wealth. An ancient house for half a million. Isam al-Baqli was born again, born again at seventy.

He enjoyed looking at his image in the old mirror: a decrepit image ravaged by time, hunger, and afflictions; the face a mold of protruding bones and repugnantly tanned skin, a narrow sunken forehead, and lackluster eyes with but a few lashes remaining; black front teeth and no molars; and a skinny, wrinkled neck. What is left of life after seventy? Yet despite everything the fortune that had alighted upon him carried an intoxication that would not evaporate. Innumerable things must be achieved. Isam al-Baqli, indigent loafer, was now Isam al-Baqli, millionaire. All those old friends who were still in the land of the living were exclaiming, "Have you heard what's happened to Isam al-Baqli?" "What's happened to the layabout?" "The house has been bought by one of those big new companies for half a million." "Half a million!" "I swear it by the Koran!"

Consternation spread through Sakakini, Qubeisi, and Abbasiyya like a hurricane. The house, with its spacious courtyard, faced onto Qushtumur Street. He had inherited it from his mother, who had passed on ten years ago after old age had turned her into a wreck. She had clung doggedly to life until the threads had been ripped to pieces and she had tumbled down. He had not grieved for her—life had accustomed him not to grieve for anything.

The family had had nothing except for his mother's small pension and the roof over their heads. He had had no success at school, had learned no trade, had never done any work—a good-for-nothing loafer. He might win a few piasters at backgammon through cheating and the indulgence of numerous friends won at school, or friends who had been neighbors in the days of childhood, boyhood, and youth. He possessed a certain charm that made amends for his many bad attributes and made one forgive him his faults, and his extreme wretchedness and the hopelessness of his situation always excited people's sympathy. His father had been an employee in the post office, and his mother had inherited the one-story Qushtumur house with its spacious and neglected courtyard. He was entitled to say that he was the son of a good family but had been unlucky, though the fact was that he was stupid, lazy, and ill-mannered, and it was not long before he was expelled from school. Practically his whole life was spent in the Isis Café, either in debt or in the process of settling his debts through cheating and the generosity of friends. His friend the lawyer Othman al-Qulla thought about taking him into his office on Army Square, but al-Baqli, with his absolute loathing for work, refused.

When left on his own after his friends had gone off to their jobs, he would spend his time indolently daydreaming. At election festivities and at weddings and funerals, he would indulge himself a little. His whole life he had lived off his charm and his friends' generosity; he made a profession of poking fun, singing, dancing, and cracking jokes in order to earn himself a meal of beans, a piece of sweet basbousa, or a couple of drags of hashish.

His natural impulses had remained starved, repressed, crazed. The Qushtumur house knew no food but beans (and the various dishes made from beans), eggplant, and lentils. As for his dreams, they revolved around fantasies of mysterious banquets and repressed sex. There were stories about his affairs with widows, divorcees, and married women too, but no one believed him, though no one called him a liar. The story everyone did believe was of his affair with a widowed servant woman ten years his senior, an affair that had quickly turned to discord and strife when it became clear that she was of a mind to marry him. In fact she had also stipulated that he find himself a job because, as the saying goes, idle hands are unclean. The affair broke up after a row in which humiliating blows were exchanged. That was the only real affair he had had, and his neighbor Mr. Othman al-Qulla had been a witness to the fight and had recounted it at the café. "You missed a scene better than a circus. A woman as fat as a sack of coal bawling out our dear friend al-Baqli and making him a public spectacle in the courtyard of his gracious house and within sight and earshot of his gracious and dismayed mother. The battle wasn't over till he was at his last gasp and some kind folk had intervened—when right away a new battle started up with his mother herself!"

Apart from that dismal experience, he would become boggle-eyed as he gawked at the women walking in the street, his heart suffering emotional pain as his stomach suffered hunger. He found no one but his mother on whom to vent his fury and frustration, despite her great love for him, the love of an old woman for an only son. Whenever she urged him to take a job or pull himself together, he would challenge her, "And when are you going to depart this world?"

"May God forgive you," she would say with a smile. "And what would you do if my pension was no longer available to you?"

"I'd sell the house."

"You wouldn't find anyone to buy it for more than five hundred pounds, which you'd fritter away in a couple of months, and you'd then take up begging."

He never said a kind word to her. His friends advised him to change his manner so he would not kill her off with worry and grief and actually expose himself to beggary. They reminded him of God's words and of what the Prophet had said about respect for one's parents, but his feeling of utter hopelessness had plucked out the roots of faith from a heart brimful with hunger and afflictions. He stuck to his scoffing, embittered attitude toward the events that passed by him, such as the battles between the political parties and the World War, calling down upon the world, with exaggerated mockery and scorn, yet more ruin and destruction. His mother completely despaired of him and resigned herself to the will of God. Sometimes, overwhelmed by distress, she would say, "Why do you repay my love with disrespect?"

And he would say derisively, "One of the causes of ill-fortune in this world is that some people live longer than necessary."

The cost of living continued to rise. Was there to be further deprivation? And so he suggested to his mother that he should take in a person, or a family, as lodgers in his bedroom and that he should sleep on the couch in her room. "And open our house to strangers!" cried his mother in disbelief.

"Better than dying of hunger," he shouted at her. He cast a glance at the courtyard of the house and muttered, "It's like a football ground and it's good for nothing."

An agent brought along a student from the country, who took the room for a pound. Friends made a joke of the incident and said that the Qushtumur house had become a boardinghouse, and they gave his mother the name "Madame al-Baqli." But he did not try to evade their ridicule and would sing "Days arrive when a man of breeding is humiliated."

Unlike many he made light of the air raids. He never responded to the siren—he would not leave his seat at the café and did not know the way to the shelter. He did not mind this. What he did mind was that life was rushing past him and he was approaching his forties without having enjoyed a decent meal or a beautiful woman. He had not even been affected by the Revolution. "It seems," he had remarked ironically, "that this Revolution is directed against us landlords!"

He never in his life read a newspaper, and got his information haphazardly at the gatherings of his friends. He became older, passed fifty. His mother became advanced in years; she grew frail and began to lose interest in things. She became critically ill. A doctor friend of his examined her and diagnosed a heart condition and prescribed medicines and rest. Rest, however, was out of the question, and medicines not feasible. In the meantime he continued to wonder how he would make out if he were to be deprived of her pension. Hour by hour she drew nearer to death, until one morning he woke up to find her dead. He looked at her for a long time before covering her face. He felt that he was recollecting dimmed memories from a distant past and that he was compelled to desist from his sarcasm and to recognize that that particular moment of the morning was a sad and melancholy one.

Right away he sought out the richest of his friends, Mr. Nuh, a dealer in property, who undertook to make the necessary arrangements for the burial of the deceased, and who also warned him against selling the house if he should find himself after a while down and out in the street. Isam al-Baqli wondered, though, how long cheating at backgammon and the letting out of the room would support him. Might there not be too a limit to one's friends' generosity? He made a venture into begging in the outskirts of the city, and it was not a barren exercise.

Days followed one upon the other, one leader died and another took his place, and then the "open-door" policy came in when he was knocking on seventy, his seventieth year of desperation and the squandering of life. The cost of living continued to rise in real earnest, and the scales wavered perilously. Begging was no longer of any avail, the generosity of friends was suddenly cut off (some of his friends had, for his bad luck, departed this world, while the remainder had betaken themselves to a quiet old age in which they were happy to sit around and chat), and he plunged headlong into the abyss of ruin. What a wretched, desperate old man he was!

Then one day the darkness of his existence dissolved to reveal the face of the broker making his descent on angelic wings straight down from the heavens. In the presence of his two friends, the lawyer and the property dealer, the transaction was concluded and the fabulous sum deposited in the bank. The three of them then sat in a low-class café on al-Azhar Street, a café whose unpretentiousness was in keeping with the wretched appearance of the millionaire. Isam al-Baqli gave a deep sigh of satisfaction that dispensed with any words. For the first time in his life he was totally happy. Yet, feeling at a loss, he said, "But don't you two leave me on my own."

"From today on you're not in need of anyone," said Othman al-Qulla, the lawyer, laughing.

But Mr. Nuh said, "He's mad and needs someone to guide him at every step."

"You two," said al-Baqli gratefully, "are the best persons I've known in my life."

"There are certain priorities," said Mr. Nuh, "before we get down to any work—things that can't be put off. First and foremost, you must go to the Turkish baths and get rid of all that accumulated dirt so that you can show your true self."

"I'm afraid they won't know me at the bank. . . ."

"And have a haircut and a shave, and today we'll buy you a ready-made suit and other clothes so that you can put up at a decent hotel without arousing suspicion."

"Shall I stay at a hotel permanently?"

"If you want to," said the lawyer. "You'll find full service and everything. . . ."

"A flat also has its merits," said Mr. Nuh.

"But a flat's not complete without a bride!" exclaimed al-Baqli.

"A bride?"

"Why not? I'll not be the first or last bridegroom at seventy!"

"It's a problem."

"Don't forget the bridegroom's a millionaire."

"That's a strong incentive, but only to the unscrupulous. . . ." said the lawyer, laughing.

"Scrupulous or not—it's all one in the end!" said al-Baqli scornfully.

"No, you might find yourself back at begging quicker than you imagined," said Nuh.

"Let's put that off for the time being," said the lawyer.

"The question of a woman cannot be put off," said Isam al-Baqli. "It's more important than the ready-made suit."

"There are plenty of opportunities, and nightclubs galore."

"My need of the two of you in this respect is particularly urgent."

"But we said goodbye to riotous living ages ago."

"How can I get along on my own?"

"Someone accompanied by money is never alone."

"We'll have another session," said Mr. Nuh, "after giving thought to the investing of the fortune. It would be wise to spend from the income and not from the capital."

"Remember," protested al-Baqli, "that I'm in my seventies and have no one to inherit from me."

"Even so!"

"The great thing is for us to make a start," said the lawyer.

When they got together in the evening, Isam al-Baqli had a new look and a new suit. But while the filth had vanished, the signs of the wretchedness of old age and former misery still remained.

"Valentino himself, by the Lord of the Kaaba!" said the lawyer, laughing.

As Othman al-Qulla was on friendly terms and had business with the manager of the Nile Hotel, he rented a fine room there for al-Baqli, and the latter at once invited his two friends to dinner. They had a few drinks before the meal and then sat together after eating, planning a meeting for the following day. Then al-Baqli accompanied them to Mr. Nuh's car but did not return to the hotel. Instead he took a taxi to Mohammed Ali Street and made straight for a restaurant famous for its Egyptian cooking. He did not consider what he had just eaten a meal, but merely something to whet his appetite. He ordered hot broth with crumbled bread and the meat of a sheep's head, and ate to his heart's content. He left the place only to pick and choose among such sweets as baseema, kunafa, and basbousa, as though afflicted by a mania for food. Just before midnight he returned to the hotel, so drunk with food he was nearly passing out. Locking his room, he experienced an unexpected feeling of sluggishness creeping through his limbs. Still with his trousers and shoes on, he threw himself down on the bed without turning off the light. What was it that lay crouched on his stomach, chest, and heart? What was it that stifled his breathing? Who was it that grasped his neck? He thought of calling for help, of searching for the bell, of using the telephone, but he was quite incapable of moving. His hands and feet had been shackled, his voice had gone. There was help, there was first aid, but how to reach them? What was this strange state he was in that wrested from a man all will and ability, leaving him an absolute nothingness? So, this is death, death that advances with no one to repulse it, no one to resist it. In his fevered thoughts he called upon the manager, upon Nuh, upon Othman, upon the fortune, the bride, the woman, the dream. Nothing was willing to make answer. Why, then, had this miracle taken place? It doesn't make sense. It doesn't make sense, O Lord.

Arabic Text Sources

Arabic text sources for the stories in this volume are as follows: "Zaabalawi," as "Za'balawi," and "By a Person Unknown," as "Didd Majhul," in *Dunya Allah (God's World),* Cairo, Maktabat Misr, 1962.

"The Conjurer Made Off with the Dish," as "al-Hawi khataf al-tabaq," and "At the Bus Stop," as "Tahta al-mizalla," in *Tahta al-mizalla (Under the Shelter),* Cairo, Maktabat Misr, 1969.

"The Answer Is No," as "'Indama yaqul al-bulbul la," "Half a Day," as "Nisf yawm," "The Lawsuit," as "al-Qadiya," "A Day for Saying Goodbye," as "Yawm al-wida'," "His Majesty," as "Mawlana," and "A Long-Term Plan," as "Khitta ba'idat al-mada," in *al-Fajr al-kadhib (The False Dawn),* Cairo, Maktabat Misr, 1989.

"The Time and the Place," as "al-'Ain wa-al-sa'a," "Blessed Night," as "al-Layla al-mubaraka," in *Ra'aytu fi ma yara al-na'im (I Saw in My Dreams),* Cairo, Maktabat Misr, 1982.

"The Ditch," as "al-Khandaq," and "The Norwegian Rat," as "al-Fa'r al-norwiji," in *al-Tanzim al-sirri (The Secret Organization)*, Cairo, Maktabat Misr, 1984.

"The Tavern of the Black Cat," as "Khammarat al-qitt al-aswad," and "The Wasteland," as "al-Khala'," in *Khammarat al-qitt al-aswad (The Tavern of the Black Cat),* Cairo, Maktabat Misr, 1969.

"The Empty Café," as "al-Qahwa al-khaliya," "Fear," as "al-Khawf," "A Fugitive from Justice," as "al-Harib min al-i'dam," in *Bayt sayyi' al-sum'a (House with a Bad Name),* Cairo, Maktabat Misr, 1965.

"The Man and the Other Man," as "al-Rajul wa-al-akhar," in *al-Hubb fawqa hadabat al-haram (Love on the Pyramid Hill),* Cairo, Maktabat Misr, 1979.

About the Author

Certainly the most world-renowned of Arabic novelists, Naguib Mahfouz was born in Cairo in 1911 and began writing when he was seventeen. A student of philosophy and an avid reader, he has been influenced by many Western writers, he says, including Flaubert, Zola, Camus, Dostoevsky, and, above all, Proust. Awarded the Nobel Prize for Literature in 1988, Mahfouz has more than thirty novels to his credit, among them his masterwork, *The Cairo Trilogy*. He lives in the Cairo suburb of Agouza with his wife and two daughters.

About the Translator

Born in Vancouver, Denys Johnson-Davies began studying Arabic at the School of Oriental Studies, London University, and later took a degree at Cambridge. He has been described by Edward Said as "the leading Arabic-English translator of our time," and has published nearly twenty volumes of short stories, novels, and poetry translated from modern Arabic literature. He lives much of the time in Cairo.

Modern Arabic Writing
from the American University in Cairo Press

Ibrahim Abdel Meguid *The Other Place • No One Sleeps in Alexandria*
Yahya Taher Abdullah *The Mountain of Green Tea*
Leila Abouzeid *The Last Chapter*
Salwa Bakr *The Wiles of Men*
Mohamed El-Bisatie *Houses Behind the Trees • A Last Glass of Tea*
Fathy Ghanem *The Man Who Lost His Shadow*
Mourid Barghouti *I Saw Ramallah*
Tawfiq al-Hakim *The Prison of Life*
Taha Hussein *A Man of Letters • The Sufferers • The Days*
Sonallah Ibrahim *Cairo: From Edge to Edge • Zaat*
Yusuf Idris *City of Love and Ashes*
Denys Johnson-Davies *The Naked Sky: Short Stories from the Arab World*
Said al-Kafrawi *The Hill of Gypsies*
Naguib Mahfouz *Adrift on the Nile*
Akhenaten, Dweller in Truth • Arabian Nights and Days
Autumn Quail • The Beggar
The Beginning and the End • The Cairo Trilogy:
Palace Walk • Palace of Desire • Sugar Street
Children of the Alley • The Day the Leader Was Killed
Echoes of an Autobiography • The Harafish
The Journey of Ibn Fattouma • Midaq Alley • Miramar
Respected Sir • The Search • The Thief and the Dogs
The Time and the Place • Wedding Song
Ahlam Mosteghanemi *Memory in the Flesh*
Abd al-Hakim Qasim *Rites of Assent*
Lenin El-Ramly *In Plain Arabic*
Rafik Schami *Damascus Nights*
Miral al-Tahawy *The Tent*
Fuad al-Takarli *The Long Way Back*
Latifa al-Zayyat *The Open Door*